SECOND CHANCE TROUBLE

By
Alex McAnders

McAnders Books

*****

The characters and events in this book are fictitious. Any similarity to real persons, living or dead, is coincidental and not intended by the author. The person or people depicted on the cover are models and are in no way associated with the creation, content, or subject matter of this book.

All rights reserved. No part of this book may be reproduced in any form or by any electronic or mechanical means, including information storage and retrieval systems, without permission in writing from the publisher, except by a reviewer who may quote brief passages in a review. For information contact the publisher at: McAndersPublishing@gmail.com.

Copyright © 2023

Official Website: www.AlexAndersBooks.com
Podcast: BisexualRealTalk
Visit Alex Anders at: Facebook.com/AlexAndersBooks & Instagram
Get 6 FREE ebooks and an audiobook by signing up for Alex Anders' mailing list at: AlexAndersBooks.com

Published by McAnders Publishing

Titles by Alex McAnders

M/M Romance

Serious Trouble & Audiobook; Book 2 & Audiobook; Book 3 & Audiobook; Book 4 & Audiobook; Book 5; Book 6
Serious Trouble - Graduation Day; Book 2; Book 3; Book 4; Book 5
Mafia Marriage Trouble & Audiobook

*****

MMF Romance

Searing Heet: The Copier Room; Hurricane Laine & Audiobook; Book 2 & Audiobook; Book 3 & Audiobook; Book 4 & Audiobook; Book 5; Book 6

*****

Titles by A. Anders

MMF Erotica

While My Family Sleeps; Book 2; Book 3; Book 4; Book 1-4
Book 2
My Boyfriend's Twin; Book 2
My Boyfriend's Dominating Dad; Book 2

*****

MMF Romance

Until Your Toes Curl: Prequels; Book 2; Book 3; Until

Your Toes Curl
The Muse: Prequel; The Muse
Rules For Spanking
Island Candy: Prequel & Audiobook; Island Candy & Audiobook; Book 2; Book 2
In The Moonlight: Prequel; In The Moonlight & Audiobook
Aladdin's First Time; Her Two Wishes & Audiobook; Book 2 & Audiobook
Her Two Beasts
Her Red Hood
Her Best Bad Decision
Bittersweet: Prequel; Bittersweet
Before He Was Famous: Prequel; Before He Was Famous
Beauty and Two Beasts
Bane: Prequel & Audiobook; Bane & Audiobook
Bad Boys Finish Last
Aladdin's Jasmine
20 Sizzling MMF Bisexual Romances

*****

M/M Erotic Romance

Their First Time
Aladdin's First Time; Her Two Wishes & Audiobook; Book 2 & Audiobook

*****

Suspense

The Last Choice; Dying for the Rose
It Runs

*****

Titles by Alex Anders

MMF Erotica

While My Family Sleeps; Book 2; Book 3; Book 4; Book 1-4
Dangerous Daddy's Double Team & Audiobook; Book 2 & Audiobook; Book 3 & Audiobook; Book 4 & Audiobook; Book 1-4
Black Magic Double Team & Audiobook

M/M Erotic Romance

Baby Boys
Baby Boy 1: Sacrificed; Book 2; Book 3; Book 4; Book 1-4

MMF Romance

As My Rock Star Desires; Book 2; Book 3; Book 4; Book 5

SECOND CHANCE TROUBLE

Chapter 1

Merri

"You've made a fool of my team, my organization, your father, and worst of all me," the red faced old man said as his strings of spider veins brightened and crawled under his ridiculous looking white goatee.

Lowering my head, I allowed my mind to drift into another world. Have you ever had a dream about doing something? It could be achieving a goal, or to make a parent proud of you.

Perhaps after a lifetime of disappointing your father, your dream was to be his assistant coach as he coached his team to an NFL championship. Just as the clock counts down, he turns to you for the play that will win the game. And having waited for this your entire life, you pull out what you've been working on for months.

"A hail Mary pass?" He'd say to you.

"It will work, Coach," you'd tell him unsure of yourself but sure that it was the right call.

"I don't know about this. The game is on the line."

"Trust me, Coach," you implore.

When he looks away with doubt, you grab his shoulder and say, "This will work, Dad."

And because of a lifetime of working together, he puts the championship in your hands and calls to the quarterback who initiates your play.

As the players blitz and settle, the quarterback launches the ball. Airborne, it travels 30, 40, 50 yards. And just as you drew it up, the receiver shakes off his defender, leaps, and then snatches it out of the air, falling into the end zone and winning the game.

Cheers and streamers follow. The other coaches lift you onto their shoulders victorious. And your father, who might have had his doubts about you, looks you in the eyes and nods as if to say, that's my son and I'm proud. ...Or, you know, some less oddly specific dream than that.

Well, I'm not too proud to admit that that might have been my dream. I've never been my father's favorite. You might even say that my father thinks of me as a bit of a disappointment.

Yes, I am my father's assistant coach. And after having a stellar Division 2 coaching career, the miracle that is 'being offered an NFL team' occurred. But that is where my dream ends. Because after two years of circling the drain, my father's career might be over before it really started.

Worse than that, as we played our last game of the season, the one that determined our playoff chances, my father ignored me completely and called a play that lost us the game.

That was fine. Our team was used to losing. It is what it is. But suddenly unburdened by game preparation and everything else football, something else found its way into my mind. After months of ignoring my boyfriend, I remembered that our relationship was on the rocks. Like my father's coaching career, it was circling the drain.

With those thoughts overwhelming me, something unexpected happened, my face appeared on the giant screen. This had happened before. When games are televised, the cameramen are always looking for reaction shots.

The only problem this time was that they had chosen to focus on me because, like a world-class homo, I was crying. I hadn't even realized it. And if you've ever thought that there was no crying in baseball, I can assure you that, unless your son just won you the NFL championship, there is definitely no crying in football.

"You fuckin' cried? On my football field? What type of god damn queer bullshit is that?"

The team's manager looked at the team's owner knowing he had just crossed a line. Of course, he didn't say anything about it. The team's owner might as well have had his hand up the manager's ass for how much of puppet the manager was.

"You're an embarrassment to my team. And that is saying a lot considering how much of a fuckin' embarrassment this whole season has been. But do you know why it's been an embarrassment? I said, do you know why it's been an embarrassment?" He asked me.

"Because our blitzing is weak. We're not deep enough to compensate for injuries. And our quarterback can't complete a pass to save his life?"

The 72 year old man sneered at me with disgust.

"No, you piece of shit, know-it-all, pillow muncher. You god damn, fuckin' pansy ass, Mary. It's because your father is surrounded by shit-for-brain assistants who would prefer to stare at the players in the shower than coach a football game."

Prickles of heat crawled through me. Every muscle in my chest clenched making it hard to breathe. He had found it. The thing I have always feared hearing the most, he had spit at me like venom.

I wasn't always open about being gay. I was the son of a football coach. Working for my father since I was a kid, I joined him in locker rooms. There were times when he would give his end of game talk with half the team naked. That's just what happened in football whether it was at the college level or the pros.

So, would things change if everyone knew I was gay? I certainly wouldn't be welcome in a locker room. Trust was an important part of game. We had to trust that the players prepared themselves adequately for every game. And the players had to trust that we weren't staring at their swinging dicks and jacking off to the thought of them when we were alone at night.

In short, gays weren't welcome in football. But here I was, the openly gay son of a losing coach whose crying had been broadcasted to every television in America. I felt humiliated.

For so long I had tried to be the man my father had wanted me to be. For so long I had laid in bed dreaming about my father finally treating me like he was proud instead of embarrassed of me. Yet time and again, I kept letting him down.

I missed things I should have noticed. I cried on national TV giving ammunition to people like the team's owner to use in exit interviews and contract negotiations.

As I felt the tears threatening again, I did everything I could to hold them back. I couldn't cry. Not now. Not here. I had to make it through this like a man. I had to be the son my father wanted me to be.

So, as the owner berated my sexuality, and my intelligence, doing everything he could to make me quit, I bit my lip. I wiggled my toes. I did everything I could to distract myself from the thought that sat in the back of my mind, 'what he said about me was right. I didn't belong here'.

'Don't cry, Merri. You won't cry!' I told myself desperately willing it to be true.

I could do this. I could get through this. And when I did, I'd prove that I belonged here. I'd show my father and everyone else that I wasn't a screw up. I wasn't an embarrassment.

I'll show them that I'm a person who belongs in football as much as anyone else. And as the wet streaks slowly rolled down my cheeks and broke my heart, I knew exactly how I'd do it.

Chapter 2

Claude

As early morning sunlight fanned over the mountains whitening the clouds, a mist filled the air. Stretching out my hamstrings one last time, I took a deep breath and began my run. Falling into rhythm in both breathing and pace, my mind settled. This morning was it. I had thought about doing it for so long and today was the day.

Rounding the mountain roads and entering the neighborhood, I went over my plan again. This was where Cage began his run. Casually bumping into him, I would invite him to join me and then do it.

There was no question that something in my life had to change. When I had first come back home, I had enjoyed the isolation. I had needed time to think. But two years of it have been too much.

Yes, I had my Facetimes with Titus and Cali, but they weren't enough. If anything, getting to know my new brothers had been what was awakening this. I wanted to be more social. I was beginning to need it.

Why had I chosen to approach Cage?

It was because we were at a similar stage in life. Since graduating from university two years earlier, we had made similar choices. Out of everyone in this small town, he was the one I could most easily see as a friend.

Besides, he and his boyfriend were the center of my brothers' friend group. Cage and Quin hosted a lot of game nights. When Cage had first moved to town, he had invited me. But after turning down one too many, the invitations had stopped.

Step one, bump into Cage. Step two, invite him to join me on my run. Step three, casually bring up game night and express an interest in joining them. It seemed so simple. Yet, it was only now, weeks after coming up with the plan, that I had mustered the courage to try.

Perhaps this was what finding yourself at the end of your rope looked like, an early morning jog meant to ask for something you desperately missed, human connection and a friend.

Doing my best not to over think this, I picked up my pace and rounded the neighborhood streets. With my heart thumping, Cage's house came into view. I had timed it correctly, I could see Cage stretching on the driveway.

As I stared, my chest hurt. Caught under an avalanche of panic, I struggled to breathe.

I couldn't do this. Not now. Not today. And just as Cage looked up noticing me jogging up his street, I turned around. Changing direction as if it had always been my plan, I jogged in the opposite direction.

I was a coward. There was no doubt about it. But worse than that, I was alone and would continue to be alone. Why couldn't I get out of this? What was wrong with me?

Returning home and heading upstairs into the shower, I stood naked with the water pooling in my curly hair. How had I become this person? University had been so different. I had had friends and a life. Now, back home in small town Tennessee, I was…

"Come down stairs when you're done," my mother said knocking on the bathroom door. "I have a surprise for you."

Snapped back to the here and now, I looked up. My mother had a surprise for me? What did she mean by that?

Shutting off the water and getting dressed, I opened the bathroom door. Immediately the smell of roasting Arabica beans hit me. God was it good. But I hadn't set it to brew.

"Surprise!" my mother said after I headed downstairs and entered the kitchen.

In one of her hands was a coffee mug. In the other was a muffin with a lit candle stuck in it.

"What's this?"

"We're celebrating," my mother said enthusiastically, with her brown skin aglow from the candlelight.

"What are we celebrating?" I asked wondering if I had forgotten a birthday.

"We're celebrating you moving into your new shop."

I smiled despite myself.

"It's really not that big of a deal, Momma."

"Of course, it's a big deal. You've worked out of our living room for the last year, and now you're going to have your own office. "

"Which I'll be sharing with Titus," I reminded her.

"What does that matter? You're now a thriving business owner and you have your own office."

"That I share."

"Claude, take the muffin," she said handing it to me. "And the coffee. I asked Marcus what type you like. He told me it's your favorite."

I smiled. "Thank you, Momma."

"You're welcome," she said with a smile. "I have a few minutes before we have to leave, why don't we sit down and enjoy a coffee together."

"Uh oh," I said taking a seat.

"What, uh oh? There's no uh oh. Can't a mother spend a few minutes sitting with her handsome son?"

"Of course, Momma," I said settling down. "Sorry. What do you want to talk about?"

Momma looked at me devilishly.

"Well, since you asked, are there any girls in your life that you'd like to tell me about?"

"Momma!"

"Or guys. I know how everyone's bisexual nowadays."

"Momma, what makes you think I'd ever be into something like that?"

She gave me a side eye that asked who I thought I was fooling.

"No Momma, there are no girls or guys in my life right now."

"And why not?" She said leaning forward.

"I can feel a lecture coming on."

"There's no lecture. I'm just gonna say…"

I groaned.

"I'm just gonna say that you're smart, and kind, and now you're a business owner."

"Here we go."

"There's no reason you shouldn't have people beating down your door."

"Maybe I don't want people beating down my door."

"Your momma had boys beating down her door," she said proudly.

"And on the topic of things I didn't need to know…"

"You should be grateful your momma was hot."

"Momma!"

"Where do you think you got your good looks from?"

"I think this conversation's over," I said getting up.

"It's over when you bring some hot piece of something home to meet me. I was sneaking boys into my room from the time I could get them through my window. Why isn't Marcus ever crawling out of your window?"

I turned to her. "I'm on the second floor!"

"Claude, you need to open yourself up to people. Everyone likes you. Just give someone a chance. You're too young and good-looking to be a lonely, old man," she told me as I took my coffee and headed upstairs to my room.

Closing the door behind me, I had to admit she wasn't entirely wrong. I mean, she was wrong about the bisexual thing, and Marcus. He was just my coffee supplier. But she was right that something needed to change.

This was not the life I had pictured for myself when I graduated university. Sure, I had what was becoming a thriving business, and I worked with Titus. But that was only spring through fall. The rest of the year, having coffee at Marcus's popup was the only time I didn't feel empty. Something had to change.

Waiting for my usual five minutes before we had to go, I headed back downstairs grabbing the car keys. With my mother at school all day, we shared a car. It worked out well considering I never went anywhere at night. But driving her this morning with her picking up her lecture where she had left off, I second guessed our arrangement.

Dropping Momma off and heading to my new place, I pulled into the parking lot and sat. Staring at the small log structure, I was expecting to feel more than I did. Momma wasn't wrong, having an office to run our business out of was a reason to celebrate. But with my business partner still finishing his spring semester, I was the only one here.

Getting out of the car, I walked the dirt path to our front door. The place was the ultimate cabin in the woods. Surrounded by perfect pines still damp with morning dew, I glanced through the trees at the shallow river less than a hundred feet away.

This place had been an excellent find. The only thing that it would never have was foot traffic. But with our tour's path beginning less than a quarter mile away, it would allow us to fit more tours into our day. The rental made a lot of sense.

Unlocking the door and looking around, I felt its vacancy. Had this been a good idea? How much more isolation did I need? Could I spend the rest of my life working here in this town?

Quickly wiping a tear from my cheek, I straightened up and got sensible. I had wanted a business and now I had it. If I wanted to open up and let someone into my life, I could do that too.

I could no longer doubt that I needed it. There was a part of me that felt like I was going to crack without it. I just had to figure out how to unclamp the hands hiding my heart.

I didn't know why I always withdrew from people the way I did, but I was going to break through that. I was going to let someone in and together we would be happy.

I could do this. I had to do this. And as I wiped another tear from my cheek, I heard a knock on the door that turned me around.

"Merri!" I said, shocked to see his steel-gray eyes once again looking back at me.

Chapter 3

Merri

"Hey Claude," I said as if it hadn't been two years since I had seen him.

God, did he look good. It wasn't like I had forgotten how his gorgeous eyebrows framed his square jaw and full lips. It was more that, I had forgotten how staring at them made me feel.

Seeing him for the first time freshman year was the final thing I needed to convince me I wasn't straight. The man's complexion was the color of milk chocolate. How could someone not want to lick it?

Claude shook his head as if he couldn't believe what he was seeing.

"What are you doing here?" He asked stunned.

"I was in the neighborhood. Thought I would stop by."

"You're in Tennessee!" He said still trying to piece everything together.

"What? Does Tennessee not have neighborhoods?" I joked.

"No, I mean, you live in Oregon."

"Actually, I'm in Florida now."

"Which still isn't near Tennessee."

I smiled. "You got me."

"So, why are you here?"

"I thought I would stop by and say hi."

"I got the keys to this place yesterday."

"Is the place new?" I said looking around at the small cabin. "You run one of those river rafting tour companies, right?"

"Yeah. How did you know?"

"You have a website," I told him as I explored the place.

"Of course. And I put this address on it."

"Bingo."

"Okay, that explains how you found the place. But that doesn't tell me what you're doing here."

I looked back at my old friend wondering which I should go into first. A lot had gone on between us before he told me he was choosing to graduate early and leave the team. And I'll admit that I didn't handle his leaving well.

"I'm here because I have a proposal for you," I said with a smile.

"And what's that?"

"I don't know if you know this, but my father became the head coach with the Cougars."

"I didn't know that," he said in a way that told me that he also didn't care.

"Okay. He did. And I became his assistant."

"Like at university?"

"Sure. Although the pros are really different. If I told you some of the things…" I looked up and paused at the sight of his uncaring eyes. I looked down. "Not the point."

"What is your point?" He asked coldly.

"My point is that he got that head coaching position, in part, because of you."

"I see."

"You aren't surprised by that?"

"We had a good season."

"We had three good seasons. And all of them were thanks to you."

"I still don't know what you're doing here."

With the moment at hand, I struggled to breathe. "I'm here because I'm inviting you to a workout."

"A what?" Claude said caught off guard.

"You know, a try out for the team."

Claude's tension dropped.

"For the Cougars?" He asked confused.

"Yeah," I said excitedly. "Papa knows that he owes a lot of his success to you, and he thinks you have what it takes to play in the pros."

"Merri, I haven't touched a football since…" he looked away to remember.

"Since you won us our third division title?"

"Yeah."

"You just put it down and never picked it back up, huh?"

"What was the point?"

"Don't you miss it? You were so good out there. The way you could find a pocket and wait until the perfect moment to throw the pass…? It was amazing."

"It's a part of my past."

"But, it doesn't have to be. I'm here telling you that if you want it, you could have it again. I'm offering you an invitation back into it. I know you loved it. I'm sure you would love it again," I said wondering if I was still talking about football.

Claude stared at me not expressing much. I could feel my confident persona melting under the heat of his gaze. He always had a way of seeing through me. I wasn't sure how he did it.

"Look, Claude," I said looking everywhere but in his eyes, "I know I don't have the right to ask anything from you, especially because of the way things ended between us. But, it would mean a lot to me if you considered this. I'm really not in a good position right now with the team…"

"So, this is about you?"

"This is about us... I mean, what we had. We had a good thing going back then, right? I was your quarterback coach and trainer. You were the star player. You shined and everyone loved you."

"That's not why I played."

"Then, why did you play?" I asked sensing a way in.

"It doesn't matter. That part of my life is over."

"But it doesn't have to be. Again, I know you don't owe me anything. But I'm asking you to at least consider it. It would mean a lot to me. Papa too. We would both love to work with you again. And, two years or not, I know that what you had is still in there. You were just that good," I said ending with a smile.

I could tell I got through to him when his gaze finally lowered.

"I'll consider it."

Rushing forward, I threw my arms around him.

"I knew you would. I knew it," I said overjoyed. "You were great back then and you'll be great again," I told him as I released him.

"I only said I'd consider it," he said coldly.

"Of course. Right," I said pulling myself together. "I'm just really happy right now. Look, I'll be in town for a few days before I head to my next meeting. How about I call you in a day or two? We could do dinner. It'll be my treat."

"You have my number?" Claude asked confused.

"Everyone has your number."

"What?"

"It's the one from the website, right?"

"Oh. Yeah."

"Then, I have it," I said heading for the door. About to leave, I stopped. "Hey, remember sophomore year when we took that camping trip to Big Bear."

"It's hard to forget. When we arrived there was half a foot of snow on the ground. It was the middle of spring."

I laughed. "Yeah. And we ended up doing a hike around that lake?"

Claude thought a moment and nodded. "When we got there it was lightly snowing."

"Remember how the sun was at a perfect angle to make the water sparkle? And do you remember the snow-topped mountains in the background."

"Yeah," he said losing himself in the thought.

"You know, I've traveled to a lot of cities since then and that is still the most beautiful sight I've ever seen. We had a few good times together, didn't we?"

Claude grunted pensively.

"I'll call you," I told him before taking a final look at my once best friend, and then walking out.

Chapter 4

Claude

I stared as my reason for leaving university early retreated to a rental car and drove away. My heart pounded. A prickling heat washed over my skin, rattling my bones. Taking a deep breath, I struggled to breathe.

I couldn't take this. Feeling caged within the office, I needed to run. I leaped to the door and flung it open. Before I knew it, I was running with all the strength and speed I had. Losing myself in the trees, all I could think about was the feeling as my leg muscles drove me forward.

I could feel the wind whip past me when I was up to speed. Around me, the world slowed down. This was how I had felt with the football in hand and a defensive line fighting to get past our offensive's wall. If I had ever had a secret weapon, it was this.

I sprinted for as long as I could. As I slowed down, I fell into a still brisk pace. I couldn't have guessed how much seeing Merri again would affect me.

At one time he had meant so much to me. But after he showed me who he really was, I had realized that I had never known him.

At university, players had joked that the reason I was so good was because I was a robot programmed to throw a football. That implied that I had no heart. I did have a heart, and it broke after the things Merri had said to me.

Exhausted and feeling like my legs were on fire, I eventually stopped. Bent over with my hands on my knees, I struggled for breath. I remembered this feeling. It was how I had felt when the loneliness got too much for me.

When the world felt like it would collapse around me, I ran. Running was the only thing that would help me do my duty. Running quieted my mind enough to be the person I had to be.

Standing as my swirling mind slowed, I looked around. I knew where I was. I was at one of the stopping points on Titus's tour. In front of me was a pond that connected to the stream that flowed by our office. Further upstream, it connected to a river that began at the mountains. With the lush green trees surrounding it, it was beautiful, peaceful.

Needing to talk to someone, I pulled out my phone and checked for a signal. Finding two bars, I called the only one I knew would answer.

"Claude, what's up?" Titus said in his usual cheerful voice.

I paused before I spoke. Why had I called him? I had needed to hear his voice? Did I just need to know that I wasn't alone?

"Claude?"

"Yeah, sorry. My phone slipped."

Titus laughed. "So, what's up?"

"Did I catch you at a bad time?"

"No. I just left class. I'm walking back to my dorm. Is Cali with you?"

"No. I was, ah, I was calling to let you know that I got the keys yesterday. We officially have an office."

"That's fantastic! Does it feel like home?" Titus joked.

"It feels like a practical space to work from," I clarified choosing my words carefully.

Titus laughed. "Of course you'd say that. Well, I'll be up tomorrow to help you move the equipment in. I'm sure Mama will be happy to have it out of the yard."

"I'm sure she will." I paused considering what I would say next. "You know, a funny thing happened when I got there this morning."

"What? Is it leaking already?"

"Nothing like that," I said as I turned to walk back to the office. "Someone was there."

"Yeah? Who? Was it a customer?"

"No. It was someone I knew from university. He was an assistant coach on the football team."

"Really? How did you know him?"

"What do you mean?"

"What do you mean, what do I mean? How did you know him?"

"He was an assistant coach on the football team and I played on the team. Although, I guess I knew him socially as well."

There was silence on the other side of the phone.

"Wait. Back up for a second there. You were on the football team at university?"

"Yeah," I said knowing that I had avoided the topic until now. "Haven't I mentioned it?"

"No you haven't mentioned it!" Titus replied stunned. "Are you telling me that in all of the time we've been working together, you've heard me talk about everything going on with my team and you never once thought to mention that you played ball at university?"

"It didn't come up," I told him.

"It didn't come up? Don't you think that's one of those things that you bring up?"

"It really wasn't a big deal. I was hoping to put that time behind me."

"Rough games, huh?"

"I guess. Anyway, the assistant coach showed up at the office. Apparently he got the address from the website."

"What did he want?"

"He wanted me to get back involved with football."

"How?"

"I'm not sure," I lied, not wanting to get into it.

"So, he just wants you back in the sport?"

"Seems like it."

"And how did you know him?"

"He was an assistant coach on the team. And, I guess you can say that we were friends."

"Friends? Wait a minute, you had friends in university?" Titus joked.

"Yes, I had friends."

"What type of friend was he? Because guys don't show up out of nowhere trying to get you back for no reason."

"I assure you, we were just friends," I said clearing up any misunderstandings. Both Titus and Cali had boyfriends, so I always felt the need to remind them that I was the straight brother.

"Doesn't sound like it," Titus teased.

"That's all we were. Though…"

I faded off.

"Don't leave me hanging."

"He and I were best friends. And there might have been a few times when he gave me the impression that he was attracted to me."

"Really? And how did you feel about him?"

"He was a friend. That's how I felt about him."

"So, this long lost friend, who you haven't talk to in how long?"

"Since I left school."

"This long lost friend who might have been into you, and who you haven't talk to in two years, shows up at your place of work trying to win you back."

"It wasn't like that."

"Are you sure? Because that's what it sounds like."

I thought about that for a moment. Titus didn't have all of the information, but was he wrong? There had been times when Merri and I were hanging out that I had caught him staring at me. It had happened more than once.

Knowing him and the circles he traveled in, I had dismissed it as him being awkward. Merri could definitely be awkward on occasion. But if he had been into me, could his invitation to workout for the team be something else? Was the workout even real?

"I don't know," I told Titus honestly.

"Well, I don't know him. But I know you. And I know that you don't know the effect you have on people. If there is a long lost best friend who has shown up out of nowhere trying to win you back, I would say, be careful.

"And, do you even want to be involved in football again? It couldn't have meant that much to you considering this is the first time you're bringing it up."

"It had its moments."

"Be careful. You might not think so, but this sounds like it has more to do with him getting into your pants than him offering you some generic football position. This sounds questionable as hell. I mean, is there really even a job?"

"Maybe you're right."

"As a guy who spent most of my life in the closet, I'm telling you I am. Unless you're looking for your first gay experience, I say pretend it never happened… And I'm not just saying that because you're my business partner and I couldn't run the business without you."

I smiled. "Of course not. Your advice isn't biased at all."

"Seriously, though. It sounds like there's more to the story than you know."

"Got it. And you're right. It does seem like there's more to the story. Maybe I'll let it go. Thanks, Titus."

"You're welcome, Bro. That's what I'm here for."

"I'll see you this weekend."

Ending the call, I considered what Titus had said. He was right about one thing. There was more to the story. Did Merri have an ulterior motive? I had always known him to be a straight forward guy. One of the things I liked best about him was that I had felt like I could trust him. That is until I couldn't.

So, did I entertain what Merri was offering? And, what exactly was he offering? When we were at school, I thought that Merri was a friend I would have for the rest of my life. He was the one guy I felt like I could be myself with.

It had been because of him that I had the success on the team that I did. In high school I had always felt the need to keep a low profile. I was the only black kid in the school and on the team. The best thing I could have done was blend in.

But during my freshman year as a walk-on, I was nervous as hell at tryouts. Throwing the ball around trying to shake off the nerves, this smaller, blonde guy with steel-grey eyes walked up to me and asked if I was trying out for quarterback. After I had told him that I played as a wide receiver in high school, he suggested that I switch positions.

I wasn't about to do that. The quarterback was the focus of the team. Not only had I never before played that position, it would require a lot more attention than I was looking for.

Keeping an eye on him as he wondered around the field, I later noticed him talking to the coach. At one point I saw both of them look at me and when it was my time to line up with the other walk-ons, coach said, "You, what's your name?"

"Claude Harper, sir."

"Merrill tells me you have an arm," he said in front of everyone.

I looked over at the guy who had seemed to be the water boy.

"I'm trying out for receiver. I have a pretty good sprint."

I had been doing a lot of running by that point. My 40 yard dash times were what I was hoping would get me on the team.

"Well now you're trying out for quarterback. You have a problem with that?"

"No, sir."

"Good. Go warm up."

I did what I was told and warmed up. I didn't know much about the team considering division two teams didn't get national coverage. But what I did know was that they were set as quarterback. Mark Thompson was a senior and was a lock to get the spot.

"I'll warm you up," Merrill told me when I headed to the nets.

"Why did you tell him that? I told you I wasn't trying out for quarterback. Are you making sure I don't get on the team?"

He looked at me startled.

"No. That's not it at all. He's my father. He told me to watch everyone and tell him what I see. I saw that you have a great arm."

"Yeah, but the team has a quarterback. You probably even have a backup."

"We have Mark. But he gets injured a lot. And our backup can't hit the side of a barn. We have fast receivers and a strong offensive line. So, if we could shore up our quarterback position, we have a chance at a division title."

"But why'd you tell your father to consider me? I told you, I don't play quarterback."

"Because you haven't played it yet doesn't mean you can't. I feel like you're one of those guys that has more going on than you let on. I know something about that."

"Yeah. You're the coach's son pretending to be the water boy."

"I am the water boy. Papa doesn't believe in giving me an unfair advantage. I have to start from the bottom like everyone else."

"Everyone else who has a job waiting for them as soon as they prove themselves?"

"What do you mean?" He asked clueless to how unlike everyone else his position was.

"Nothing."

"Well, if you want, I can run and you can hit me on the move."

"Sure," I told him sending him long.

After a few passes flew left and right of him, he came back to me.

"I told you I'm a receiver," I said hoping he would get me transferred back to where I belonged.

"Are you trying?"

"What do you mean if I'm trying? I'm throwing it, aren't I?"

"You're throwing it like someone is forcing you to try out for quarterback."

"Someone is forcing me to try out for quarterback."

"Okay, fine. But, are you telling me that that's all you have?"

"That's what I got."

"So, you're saying if your girlfriend's life was on the line…"

"I don't have a girlfriend."

"Then let's say your mom. If it meant saving your mom's life, would that be how you threw the ball? You don't have anything beyond that?"

I looked at him knowing what he was talking about. Yes, I was holding back. I always held back because you never want anyone to know what you're truly capable of. You want people to underestimate you. It was how my mother taught me to survive as the only black kid in small town Tennessee.

But staring at the guy who looked at me with unusual interest, I remembered that I was no longer in Tennessee. I was at a university in Oregon. A key to survival was being aware of your surroundings and my surroundings had changed. What did that mean for my survival?

"I might have something past that," I said bringing a smile to Merrill's face.

"Then, let me see it," he said jogging down the field.

Centering myself as he ran away, I dug deep and locked in. As soon as he turned and crossed, I let loose everything I had and hit him in the chest. It felt good.

Giving me the ball back, he ran 10 yards further and crossed again. Letting it fly, I hit him in the numbers. No matter how far away he ran, each time I landed the ball exactly where I wanted it. My play had even surprised me. Until then, I was never sure of what I was capable of. I had discovered it thanks to Merrill.

"Call me Merri," he told me as we returned to his father. "He's ready, and he's really good," Merri said enthusiastically.

"Oh yeah? Let's see it," Coach said sending me onto the field.

Sitting at my office desk, I was snapped out of the memory by a notification on my phone.

The text read, 'Hey Claude, Merri here. This is my number in case you need to get a hold of me. Let's grab a bite to eat.'

I stared at the message. Why was Merri here? Was there actually a workout? Or was there something else going on like Titus had suggested?

'Let's meet tonight. There's a diner on Main Street. I'll be there at 7,' I wrote back.

It wasn't long before his reply arrived.

'Excellent! Can't wait. Thanks.'

My chest clenched reading it. What was it about Merri that got me to do things I didn't want to do? I didn't want the spotlight from playing quarterback. But he convinced me and we won three consecutive titles.

I had walked away from football. Yet, here I was... Hell, I didn't know what I was doing.

All I knew was that I had been happy having Merri out of my life. Well, maybe I wasn't happy, but I was figuring it out. And now, here I am excited about seeing him again.

I didn't want to be excited about seeing him. He had said awful things to me. Was I so desperate to connect with someone that I was going to overlook what he did? What he had said?

This wasn't me at all. I felt like I was slowly losing myself. Clearly Merri still had some type of power over me. And if he could convince me to ignore what happened the last time I saw him, what else could he convince me to do?

Chapter 5

Merri

I sat in my room still buzzing from seeing Claude again. I had forgotten how good he looked. I mean, he was hard to forget, but somehow he still made my heart thump. Looking at my hands, they were shaking.

No one else has ever had this effect on me. That was why I ran away from my feelings for him back at school. Every day that passed I was losing my grip on the image I had worked a lifetime to maintain.

I was the son of a football coach. All I ever wanted to do was follow in his footsteps. If I were gay, I could never have that. So I thought that if I could fight my feelings for Claude, my dreams would come true.

How had I made such a mess of things? Not able to take my mind off of Claude's text, when my phone rang, I immediately answered it.

"Hello?" I said hoping to hear his voice.

"So you decided to pick up?" the caller replied.

"Jason?" I asked.

I looked at the caller ID. It read 'Unknown'.

"Expecting someone else?"

"No, I... I was waiting for a business call."

"I bet you were," he said with the venom that had brought me to tears at the end of the last game of the season.

"I'm not cheating on you if that's what you're thinking."

"I wasn't. But it's good to know where your mind's at."

"What is it Jason?" I said not wanting to have this conversation.

"Is that how you're gonna talk to me? You leave town without telling me and that's what you're gonna say?"

"What do you want me to say?"

"How about that you're sorry? Or that you're going to stop being such a dick to me."

"I really don't have the time for this?"

"And that's the problem, you never have time for me. During the season you make the excuse that you're preparing for games..."

"I have to prepare for games!" I insisted.

"Then when the season ends, you take off without a word like I don't matter to you, even a little?"

"Of course you matter to me."

"Then why don't you act like it? Why don't you ever act like it?"

I knew the answer to that question. It was because there was always a part of me that believed I would end up with Claude. I knew it wasn't fair to Jason, but I had always had one foot out the door with him. I was never all in.

"Nothin', huh? Figures," he said after my long silence.

"What does that mean?"

"That means I don't think I want to do this anymore."

"Do what?"

"This! Any of this?"

"What are you saying?"

"I'm saying I wanna break up."

"Okay. Whatever," I told him not wanting to fight anymore.

"So that's it, huh?"

"You're the one who said you wanted to break up."

I couldn't be sure, but I thought I heard Jason begin to cry.

"Fine. Bye, Merri."

"Bye, Jason," I said ending the call.

Tears rolled down my cheeks before I could do anything to stop them. The reason I hadn't spoken to Jason before leaving was because I was trying to avoid this. The reason why my tear-stained cheeks had been broadcast nationwide was because the season was over, and I knew that we would eventually get to here.

Jason had been my first gay relationship. I had started dating him when I thought being cute and gay was enough to sustain a partnership. After a year together, I realized that it wasn't.

We were different people. If we were stereotypes, he would be the sassy, party gay while I was the closet-case. It wasn't like I was ashamed of him or anything. He was successful and hot. I just wasn't looking for our families to get together at Christmas.

The truth was that he deserved better than me. Everyone did. I was a lousy boyfriend. I worked all of the time. I didn't like PDA. And I was hung up on my straight best friend who I hadn't talked to in two years. Why would anyone want to be with me?

I sniffled and wiped the tears from my face. I had created this situation and now I had to deal with it. I had created everything bad that had happened to me recently, and I was going to have to figure my way out of it.

So although it seemed daunting, there was no better place to start than where it all began, with Claude. Knowing him, he walked away from the team and me and had never looked back.

I guess I should just be grateful that he still remembered my name. Claude had a way of blocking out anything that he didn't like. And for the past two years, I was sure that he didn't like me.

Feeling my phone buzz, I looked at it expecting it to be Jason again. It wasn't. It was a text from Papa.

'Make any progress with Claude?'

I had been honest with Claude when I told him that both Papa and I wanted him back. Sure, we each had our own reasons, but the desire was real.

If I wanted to figure my way out of the mess I was in with Claude, I was going to have to start with a few truths. Because on top of being gorgeous and a super athlete, he was also one of the smartest guys I knew.

He had to know that I wouldn't have shown up out of the blue like I had just to offer him a workout. And if I was going to go from closeted-gay to well-adjusted gay, I had a lot of work to do. That work was going to start with Claude.

Crap – why was my life always such a drama? I guess I really was a stereotype. But that ended tonight.

Chapter 6

Claude

Having arrived at the diner early, I sat at a booth that faced the wall of glass and the door. Having seen the car he had driven away in, I knew what I was looking for. When it arrived, I felt a tightness in my chest and a lump in my throat.

I didn't know why I felt like this, but I did. I would like to say that it was because of the inevitable confrontation we would have. But I knew that feeling. It would have felt like stress. I was feeling something else. Something I hadn't felt in a while.

Waving to him when he turned my way, he smiled and came over. He looked way too happy to be here. Maybe Titus was right. Maybe this conversation was going in a direction I didn't foresee. How did I feel about that?

"You're here," he said looking down at me from the other side of the table.

"I said I would be."

"You did. And, you always do what you say you're gonna do."

"I try."

Nodding with a grin on his face, Merri stared at me awkwardly.

"Are you going to sit?"

"Yeah, of course," he said sliding beside me and again being awkward. "Hey, do you remember that pizza joint we used to go to?"

"Palermo's?"

"That's right, Palermo's. We couldn't get enough of it."

"I remember. When you folded the slice, grease pooled on the cheese."

"And it wasn't just a little, either. You could fry a whole other pizza with it," he said with a laugh.

"Yeah," I said resisting his trip down memory lane. "So, is that why you suggested this, so we could talk about pizza?"

"No. No, that is definitely not why I asked you here."

"What can I get for you two?" The big bellied cook asked us.

"A burger for me, Mike."

"And for you?"

Merri retrieved the menu from its holder in the center of the table and quickly scanned it.

"You know what? I'll just have whatever he's having."

"Two burgers medium, coming up," Mike said, not writing it down.

"You know him?" Merri asked me.

"It's a small town. Everyone knows everyone."

"What's that like? Where I grew up there were just over 10,000 people. That's not a lot compared to almost anywhere else, but you can go a lifetime without meeting everyone."

"Yeah, it's a little different here. My high school had 100 students and it was the only one for 40 miles."

"So you met everyone your age on the first day of kindergarten?"

"Pretty much."

"That's wild. So, everyone knows your business?"

"It's not much they don't know."

Merri paused.

"How does that work with dating?"

"What do you mean?"

"Do all of you, like, have to take turns dating the same people?"

Against my better judgement, I laughed.

"No, there is no dating requirement here."

"But there can't be a lot of options."

"Yes, options are limited."

"So, what do you do about that?"

"Well, if you're me, you choose not to date until you get to college."

"I don't remember you dating a lot of people at school."

"Is this why you asked to talk, to find out the dating rituals of small-town America?"

Merri looked embarrassed.

"No, that's not what I wanted to talk about, either."

"Then what?"

"Do you remember that girl I was dating freshman year?"

I groaned.

"I promise you, this is going somewhere."

"Yes, I remember her. Sheryl or something. Wasn't it?"

"Yeah, Sheryl. Did I ever tell you why we broke up?"

"Wasn't it something about "not feeling it with her"?"

"Yeah. That's what I said."

"Was it not the truth?"

"No, it was true… Look, there's a reason why I broke up with Sheryl and with Angie, and with Margo. There's a reason why I broke up with all of the women I dated."

"Why's that?" I said unintentionally holding my breath.

"It was because I was interested in someone else at the time," he said looking at me vulnerably. "And I don't want to freak you out because time has passed. Things have changed."

"Why did you break up with them, Merri?" I asked suddenly really needing to know.

He took a deep breath. "The reason I broke up with all of them was because I was having feelings for someone else. And I want you to know, it's not the same now."

"Who Merri?"

"You, Claude," he said staring at me with his gentle grey eyes.

My heart pounded looking at him.

"Two burgers, medium," Mike said drawing our attention.

"Thanks, Mike," I told Titus's soon to be stepfather.

"Yes, thank you," Merri said looking away.

Neither of us looked at each other for a while. Readjusting our plates, Merri broke the silence.

"I'm gay. I wanted you to know that. I thought it was important that I put that out there."

"How long have you known?" I asked unsure what else to say to my ex-best friend who just declared that he had had feelings for me.

"How long have I known that I'm attracted to guys? Or how long have I known that I wasn't interested in women?"

I chuckled. "Both."

"Well, I knew I was attracted to guys when I started picturing Bobby Tilway naked. He was my best friend in elementary school. Believe me, no one wanted that," he joked. "And I knew I wasn't attracted to girls freshman year of college."

"What was it that told you?"

Merri moaned. "Ahh, you're gonna make me say it, aren't you?"

"Say what?"

"Fine. I knew I wasn't into girls the day I saw you at tryouts. I had had a few girlfriends in high school. But when I saw you, I realized what I was supposed to have been feeling."

"Wow!"

"Have I freaked you out?" Merri asked vulnerably.

"You haven't. But it explains a lot."

"I bet it does," Merri said holding his cheeks as his fair skin turned shades of red. "Listen, I'm sorry about that."

"About what?"

"About all of it."

"You couldn't help the way you felt."

"Yeah, but I didn't always handle it with your level of grace."

"Are you talking about when you flipped out on me?"

"Yeah. When I flipped out on you, otherwise known as the last time I spoke to my best friend before he left school and disappeared out of my life."

"I remember it well."

"I said some stuff."

"You did."

"But now I can tell you the real reason I got so upset. It was because I had finally hit a point when I couldn't pretend any more. I was…" he nodded his head to soften his words, "in love with my best friend, the star player on my dad's football team, on which I was the assistant coach."

"You had a lot of things going on," I said not knowing what else to say.

"There were a few things," he said looking mortified. "So when you then informed me that you were choosing to take early graduation, I didn't handle it well."

"You called me a "fucking ni…"."

"Please don't say it," he said cutting me off with his eyes closed and his face turning beet red. "I know what I said. And I'm so, soooo, sorry."

"You know, I've thought a lot about what you said since then. What I could never understand is why you went straight to race."

"Because I'm a fucking asshole," he said, unable to look at me.

"No, I'm serious. You had never brought up race before. Not once. But in that moment you went straight there. Why?"

"There is no excuse but I was in a lot of pain. What you said devastated me and you said it to me like you didn't give a shit about how I felt. So, I said the thing I thought would hurt you the most."

I thought about that.

"You know, when I was kid, and I'm talking 8-years-old, I was at a classmate's birthday party. After the cake and the ice cream we were all running around like chickens with our heads cut off. We were all screaming like banshees and at one point my mother pulled me aside.

"Getting down to my level, she pointed out something I hadn't noticed up to that point. She made me understand that not only was I the only black kid in my class, but I was the only black kid in the town.

"She told me that although the white kids could run around acting a fool like that, I couldn't. As the only black kid for 40 miles, all of the white kids were going to look at me and judge my entire race by what I did. She said that I could never be like them. I always had to be better.

"I carried that for a long time. It really shaped me. But then I went to university and I made a friend who race didn't seem to matter to. He told me that I shouldn't hide who I was. I shouldn't hold back.

"And then after learning to trust him and beginning to share things with him that I hadn't with anyone, he reminded me that, even to those where race didn't seem to matter, I would always just be a…"

"Don't say it. Please don't say it," Merri begged.

"…Fucking nigger."

He lowered his head as tears wetted his cheeks.

"I wouldn't blame you if you never forgave me. I wouldn't forgive me if I were you. In fact, if you want me to leave, I'll go.

"But I just want you to know that it is the most shameful thing I've ever done. No matter what I was going through, there was no excuse for what I did. If you could find it in your heart to forgive me, I would be grateful. But I don't expect you to and I wouldn't blame you if you don't. Because I wouldn't forgive me if I were in your place."

I considered that and grabbed my burger.

"You told me that you said it to hurt me. Well, you succeeded. It hurt," I admitted before taking a bite.

"I'm so sorry."

Staring at him as I chewed, I could see his shame.

It had taken a while for me to come to grips with him saying that to me. One of the ways I had had been to tell myself that he didn't understand the weight of what he had said. Because as much as me being black, or mixed, meant to me, it didn't seem to matter at all to him.

But it turns out that he did know its weight. And he had swung it like a club.

"Should I go?" Merri asked meekly.

I didn't answer because I didn't know.

"If you want, I'll go and you'll never have to hear from me again. Should I go?"

"I haven't decided."

"Okay," he replied unsure what he should do next.

When enough time passed without a word from me, he started eating his burger. Soon the two of us were eating in silence.

"So, is what you said about a workout for the Cougars real?" I asked him when my burger was gone.

"It is. Everything I told you is. Coach feels he owes his job to you and thinks you could help the Cougars."

"And, when are you leaving town for your next meeting?"

"Oh. Everything I told you is real except that," he said looking down. "To be completely honest, I'm only on this trip to see you. We think you're the team's best hope."

"I've told you that I haven't touched a football since our last game, right?" I said, considering his offer.

"If things work out, you would have the summer to get into game shape. I could help you," he offered shyly.

"I don't know."

Merri looked up at me and tilted his head questioningly. "Does that mean you're considering it?"

"I'll think about it."

Merri slumped as if relieved of a heavy burden.

"That's great, Claude. Thank you," he said gratefully. Sliding out of the booth, and putting cash on the table he added, "I'll be in town for a few days. Take the time you need. Just know that Coach and I really want you. …I mean to be a part of the team. You know, to workout."

"I got it. I'll think about it," I said tightening my lips.

Merri was about to walk away when he stopped and looked at me with vulnerable eyes.

"I've really missed you. I hope, somehow, even if you decline the workout, that we might again become friends."

"I'll think about it," I told him, for the first time in years, remembering the good times we had shared.

Chapter 7

Merri

Returning to my car, I drove until I was out of sight of the diner and then pulled over and cried. What I had said to Claude had haunted me every day since I had said it. How could I have called him that? I had loved him. I was sure that I was in love with him. Yet, I said something that hadn't crossed my mind until it was out of my mouth.

I hated myself for what I had said. I felt frozen in that moment. I was sure that was what was preventing me from moving on from my feelings for Claude. I couldn't forgive myself and I couldn't let it go.

Claude hadn't forgiven me for what had happened but at least we had talked about it. Finally my life could progress. Who was I past the person who had betrayed my best friend? I wasn't sure. But I was ready to find out.

Returning to the bed and breakfast, I headed upstairs to my room and laid in bed. After staring at the ceiling for a while exhausted, I received a text.

'Update me on what's happening with Claude,' my father wrote.

I couldn't handle this right now. Papa had no idea what happened between Claude and me. As far as he knew, at one moment Claude was his star quarterback and the next Claude was telling him that he had graduated and wouldn't be returning.

Although he never mentioned it, I was sure he knew that something had happened between us. How could he not considering that after Claude left, I couldn't look Papa in the eyes?

It wasn't long after that that I came out to him. That wasn't something I had ever planned to do. I had wanted to work in football and I had thought that coming out would end my chances. But being denied the only job I ever wanted would be my penance.

Telling him I was gay, Papa listened, told me he loved me, and then never brought it up again.

I didn't know if he was in denial, but nothing changed between us. Even when I became more public about it, he still continued conversations as we walked into the locker room and never allowed any of the players to look at me funny for being there.

After getting the head coaching job at the Cougars, there were new wrinkles. The team's owner was a fossil from another era. Papa couldn't protect me like he once had.

Being good at my job was going to have to be protection enough. Working twice as hard as everyone else allowed most people to forget that I was gay. Even the owner had to keep his bigoted comments to himself.

If only that camera hadn't caught me crying. But after coming out and being able to keep my job, maybe this was its true fallout. Would the owner have made as big of a deal about it if he had thought I was straight? Probably not. I've seen football players cry before. It happens more than you think.

Not ready to reply to Papa's text, I stuck my phone in my pocket and headed downstairs. Seeing someone in the kitchen I hadn't seen before, I guessed who it was.

"You're the son that was in New York at a funeral, right?" I asked the built, dark-haired guy who appeared to be around my age.

He didn't quite smile but it looked like he was trying to be friendly.

"I am. And I'm guessing you talked to my mother."

"Yeah, when I checked in."

"You're Merrill, right?"

"Yes. But you can call me Merri," I offered.

"Cali," he said offering me his hand.

"Nice to meet you," I said suddenly noticing how intensely good-looking he was.

"Were you close to the deceased?"

"No. It was for my partner's father. I only met him a few times."

"Do you like New York?"

"No. But that's probably just because of my partner's asshole brother."

"That's too bad."

"It takes all types in this world," he said leaving the kitchen.

Not wanting to be alone, I followed him.

"So, what's the nightlife like around here?"

Cali paused looking at me confused.

"Around here?"

"Yeah."

He laughed.

"Alright. How about anything that can take my mind off of having just broken up with my boyfriend," I said with a hint of flirtation. I had started dating Jason pretty quickly after coming out, so I still wasn't sure how hitting on guys worked.

Cali stared at me for a second and said, "I'm going to a game night in a few. My boyfriend's still in New York so the numbers will be off. Any interest in joining? It's nothing fancy."

"Yes!" I said not letting him finish. "Tell me when and where. I'll be there."

Cali's suggestion was that we drive there together. He wasn't the talkative type but he did tell me that he met his partner when his boyfriend was a guest at his bed and breakfast. Apparently there was drama surrounding it but he didn't go into the details.

Considering how small the town was, I wondered what it was like for him to be gay, or whatever he was. There couldn't be more than a few hundred people living around here. With a population that size, he had to be the only guy who dated guys for miles.

I lived in Florida and I had trouble meeting gay men. Of course, that might have had something to do with working in football, and having been in a relationship for the past year. But, I wasn't even running into gay people on a monthly basis.

Living in a place like this had to be exceptionally lonely for Cali. Even surrounded by my team and with Claude as my best friend, I couldn't deny how lonely I had felt.

I'm sure it had something to do with why I snapped. I could have been surrounded by a hundred people back then and I still would have felt breathtakingly empty. I could only imagine how Cali felt here.

Pulling into the driveway of a gorgeous two-story home, we were greeted at the door by Quin, a guy who was my size and unquestionably not straight. He owned the place along with his boyfriend, Cage, a man large enough to play football.

I was then introduced to Lou. He was Quin's unquestionable gay roommate at University. His boyfriend was running late. And after that I met Kendall whose boyfriend was upstairs.

What the hell? Was this why I never met any gays where I lived? Did they all live here?

"Where are you visiting from?" Quin asked as he handed me a drink.

"Florida."

They all looked at each other. Considering the politics in Florida, I didn't have to wonder why they had.

"It's not as bad as it seems," I said defending my new home.

Lou, who was apparently the funny one, replied, "For who? Because from here, it seems really bad. And were in Tennessee."

I looked at everyone unsure what to say.

Quin retorted, "Be nice, Lou."

Lou responded, "Lamb chop, I'm always nice."

"Be heterosexual nice," Cage joked. "Remember, he's from Florida."

Everyone laughed, including me.

Still, Cali said, "Come on guys, be gentle. He just broke up with his boyfriend."

There was a collective response of, "Ohhhh," as if my being there suddenly made sense.

"I'm sorry to hear that. Would you like to talk about it?" Kendall said with the empathy of a therapist.

"Think, off the clock, Kendall," Lou teased.

"Personal pain doesn't work on a clock," Kendall replied.

"But my drinks do. Where's the good stuff? It's got to be 2 A.M. somewhere," Lou said with a grabbing motion.

"You're in rare form," Cage said taking a swig.

"He misses, Titus," Quin explained to Cage.

"You guys go to the same school," Cage said to Lou.

"Yeah but between school, his business, and Mayoral duties, I barely see him," he said faking tears.

"That's what happens when you marry into politics," Cage quipped.

"You're married," I asked stunned.

"No," Lou said again faking tears.

Cage added, "Whatever you do, don't propose to him. He's likely to say yes."

Everyone snickered.

"That's right. Laugh at my pain. I hate you all," Lou said upset.

"But you know we love you," Quin told him, giving him a hug.

"Speaking of married," Lou began, turning the table. "When are you finally going to make an honest woman out of this one," he said to Cage.

Quin let Lou go and hunkered down by Cage's side.

"Maybe when his dad gets done writing our prenup," Cage said with a hint of tension.

"You're making him sign a prenup?" Lou asked Quin.

"My dad is before he will bless the wedding."

"Good for him," Lou responded. "You know Cage is only after you for your body, right? What if something happens between you two? Which half is he going to get?"

"Our prenup says, the bottom," Cage joked. "But I only want my baby for his brain."

"Aww, Cage," Quin said turning around and kissing his boyfriend.

Lou made a puking sound.

I turned to Cali who had been the only one not to speak. Thinking I was looking for an explanation, he said, "Quin's a genius and his father's a billionaire.

I mouthed, Wow, to him.

"We're being rude," Kendall inserted, turning to me.

Lou responded with, "We are. I'm sorry, what were we making fun of you about, again?"

I pretended not to remember.

"Don't mind him," Kendall said. "What brings you to this neck of the woods?"

"Running from the mob?" Lou asked.

That didn't get the same reaction from everyone.

"What? Too soon?" Lou asked looking around.

"Anyway," Kendall said turning everyone's attention back to me.

"I'm here for work," I explained.

"Really? What do you do?" He continued.

"I work in football."

As soon as I said it, everyone went silent. It was like I had just said that I was a cop here to raid the place.

Kendall looked at Cage and Cali. "What aspect of football?"

"I'm an assistant coach for the Cougars." When no one spoke, I asked, "Do you guys follow football?"

That was when I turned hearing someone descending the stairs. Initially I didn't recognize him, not having seen him without his shirt on. But it hit me pretty quickly. My mouth dropped open.

"What?" the guy asked the others in his, now famous, southern accent. "Who's this?" He said referring to me.

"You're Nero Roman," I said unable to help myself.

"Yeah. Who are you?" He replied with full southern twang.

"I'm Merri Hail. I work for the Cougars. And I'm a big fan."

"Who's this?" Nero asked looking around for an explanation as he joined us.

"He's staying at my place," Cali explained. "He was looking for a way to take his mind off of a break up so I invited him here. I thought he would balance out the numbers."

"I see," Nero asked staring at me as he decided something. "Anyway, are we doing this? I feel a win streak coming on. You got my back, Kendall?"

"Oh, Kendall!" I said reflexively. "You're Nero's boyfriend who's hoping to get your PhD in clinical psychology."

"Seriously, who is this?" Nero asked Cage.

"You heard it. He's Merri and he's an assistant coach with the Cougars. Why did you say you were in town?"

"I'm doing some recruiting," I said feeling my palms sweat.

Again, the room fell into silence.

With his eyes darting around the room, Cage asked, "And who are you here recruiting?"

"Oh wait! You're Cage Rucker, Nero's brother. You set a D1 record for most passes in a season."

"Yeah," Cage said modestly.

"So, who are you recruiting?" Nero asked.

I stumbled over my words. "Ah, Claude. Claude Harper. It's a small town. Maybe you know him."

The group once again looked at each other.

Nero clarified, "You said you're from the Cougars?"

"Yes."

"The NFL team?" Nero added.

"Yeah," I said confused by everyone's responses. "Do you all not know Claude?"

Nero said, "Oh, we know him. Which is why we're all a little confused."

"What do you mean?" I asked unsure what was going on. "Are you all joking again? I can't tell."

Nero looked at Cage and then Cali. All three guys' mouths were hanging open.

"Am I missing something?"

Cage gathered himself and explained.

"It's just that a few of us in this room have some experience in football. Even Cali set a record last year in yards kicked."

I turned to Cali, stunned.

"And, we all know Claude," Cage continued. "Some of us better than others. But none of us would know why there would be a recruiter from the Cougars meeting with him."

I stared at everyone confused. "You're joking again."

"No!" Nero confirmed. "I played with him in high school and we've hung out a few times since he's been back. And I have no clue what you're talking about."

I looked around baffled.

"None of you know about his records?"

Everyone looked at Cali who responded, "I didn't even know he played in college."

"So, you don't know?"

"Know what?" Cage asked.

I turned to Cage. "With all due respect, you were a good quarterback. If it wasn't for your injury, I'm sure you could have been the starting quarterback on most NFL teams. But Claude is a quarterback with generational talent."

"Claude Harper?" Nero confirmed.

"Yes."

"In high school he played wide receiver," Nero pointed out.

"I know. At tryouts I saw him throw and told the coach to test him at quarterback. He took us to three straight D2 titles."

"Claude Harper?" Nero asked again.

"Yes! You don't know how good he is. He is probably the most amazing quarterback I've ever seen in my life."

When no one responded I continued.

"Once in the conference finals, we were down by 6 and there were 20 seconds left on the clock. My dad, I mean, the coach calls out a play. He waves it off, calls different audibles for the offensive line and the receivers, and then, in the middle of everything, invents a play on the spot.

"On the sidelines, we're like, "What are you doing?" But then they hike the ball, Claude dances between the defensive line that pours through the offense like a sieve. We're thinking, he's gone. But as if a miracle, an opening the size of the red sea parts.

"How? We don't know. All we know is that Claude is suddenly running through it. And he's going and going. We thought he was gonna go all of the way until, out of nowhere, a cornerback is right on top of him.

"That's when an amazing thing happens. He fumbles the ball from contact with his own body. The ball pops up and our wide receiver, who is somehow there, scoops it into his arms and runs it into the end zone.

"The crowd went wild. The receiver was given the game ball. He became a legend for rescuing our disaster of a quarterback.

"But the thing is, the coach and I studied his play. The play Claude called would have put the receiver exactly where he needed to be to pick up a fumbled ball by a quarterback who had run the field and had accidentally made contact with the ball because of pressure from an approaching cornerback.

"The entire play was intentional! He had come up with this on the fly with 20 seconds left and the game on the line. It's beyond incredible! And that isn't even the only time," I said feeling my eyes burn and my nose getting stuffy.

"I could give you story after story of him seeming like he didn't know what he was doing, or waving off our plays and calling his own where because he did it, we won the game. Yet if you ask him if he meant to do any of it, he'll say, "No. I guess I just lucked out.""

"The man took us to three division titles. No one is that lucky. He is the most brilliant player I have ever seen in my life. And it's because of him that my father has his job and I'm an assistant coach in the NFL. He's just amazing!" I said tearing up.

There was silence.

"Claude Harper?" Nero asked again.

"Yes, Claude Harper! The amazingly brilliant Claude Harper," I told him with a teary-eyed smile.

"Shit!" Nero exclaimed.

"Did you know any of this?" Cage asked Cali.

Cali was speechless.

"I... I... No," he said looking disturbed.

"You're making this up?" Nero protested.

"No. That's why I'm here."

"So you're saying that Claude did all of this, won three national titles, and never shared a word of it to anyone?" Nero asked.

I considered his question.

"I mean, if you know Claude, I guess it's not that surprising," I conceded.

"Do you know who that is?" Nero said pointing at Cali.

"Who? Cali?"

"Otherwise known as Claude's brother," Nero explained.

"What?" I said turning towards the good-looking white guy in front of me.

"We're half-brothers," Cali explained.

"You're his brother?" I asked wondering how much he knew about me and what I had done.

"Me and Titus."

"Claude has two brothers? He never mentioned that to me," I said shaken.

"Were you two close?" Kendall asked.

"I thought we were," I said hesitantly.

"I thought we were, too," Cali replied.

"Shit, I gotta see this!" Nero said snapping out of his stupor.

"I think we all do," Cage confirmed.

I turned to them. "I've had a challenge getting him to consider my offer."

"What are you offering," Nero asked.

"A workout for the Cougars."

"What's he saying?" Cali asked.

"He says he hasn't touched a football since our last game two years ago."

"That's a real thing," Cage pointed out. "What you don't practice, you lose. Believe me, I know."

"With all due respect, Cage, Claude's talent might be on a different level." I turned to Nero. "You said he played receiver in high school, right? Because that's what he told me too. But he was such an amazing quarterback, there were times when I thought he was lying.

"If he could take a position he's never played in his life and play at that level, I don't think a two year break will make that much of a difference," I concluded to everyone.

"Cage, I've got to see this," Nero repeated.

"So do I," Cage agreed.

"How do we make this happen?" Nero questioned the group.

After a second of thought, I said, "Could you arrange a scrimmage? I bet if you got him on a field, everything would come right back to him," I told them thinking it might also help him remember the love he had for football... and me.

"I could probably do that," Cage declared. "Would you be available to play?" He asked Cali.

"Yeah, sure."

"So that's me, Nero, Cali. We could probably get Titus involved."

"You could ask a few of your players," Nero suggested.

"Your players?" I asked Cage.

"I coach the high school team. I coached Cali," Cage said with a smile.

"Oh. Cool," I said suddenly feeling very at home.

"Yeah. I'm sure a few of the players would be up for this. They've been asking me for weeks when Nero was gonna come talk to them."

"Well, now they have an assistant coach with the Cougars," Nero said gesturing to me with a smile.

"I don't know why they would want to hear from me. But if they did, I would, of course, be happy to say a few words."

"Then it's settled," Cage said. "Tomorrow Claude is going to join us for a pick-up game."

"If I know Claude, he's not gonna go for that," Cali responded. "But apparently, I don't know Claude at all. So what do I know?"

"I don't get it," I said, still very confused. "Didn't he talk about football at all when he came home for breaks?"

"They didn't know they were brothers until a few months ago," Cage explained.

"Yeah, that seems to be a thing in our town," Nero added.

"Ahhh! That makes more sense," I said feeling better about Claude not telling me.

"I think you're right, Cali," Nero agreed. "He's not gonna come if we tell him why he's coming."

"What are you suggesting?" Cage asked.

Nero replied, "Why don't we just say that we're doing a last minute thing for someone's birthday? Who has a birthday coming up?"

"Mine was last month," Cage volunteered.

"Perfect," Nero declared. "We'll say you wanted to get the guys together for a post-birthday pick-up game because you were feeling old and nostalgic for your glory days," Nero said teasing his brother.

"I turned 25," Cage protested.

"As I said, old," Nero told him with a laugh.

"I'll see you in two years," Cage said to Nero.

"You better make that three," Nero said proudly. "Don't make me sound over-the-hill like you."

Cage looked at everyone annoyed. As he did, Quin hugged him and kissed his cheek.

"Don't worry, I'll always love you."

"Thank you," he said looking at him with a smile.

"And I like being with an elderly man," Quin joked.

"What?" Nero said delighted by Quin's teasing. "Quin? Respect!"

"You too?" Cage protested.

"I'm joking."

Cage changed the topic. "Anyway, we have our plan. I'll go give Claude a call. And afterward, can we please get to playing games?" He said before leaving for a quiet room.

"Oh, now he's mad," Nero said to me. "Those two are gonna try to wipe the floor with us."

Cali explained, "When Cage and Quin play together, they're really hard to beat."

Kendall added, "Anyone plus Quin is hard to beat. I call dibs on Quin as a partner."

"You gonna abandon me just like that, boyfriend?" Nero protested hurt.

"After you riled Cage up like that? I don't want to be a part of the bloodbath that you created. I wanna win."

Everyone laughed.

"I'm supposed to be the competitive one in our relationship," Nero explained. "You're supposed to be the good person."

"I am. But I'm also smart," Kendall teased.

"I see how this goes. Don't worry, Lou and I are gonna destroy the both of you," Nero said wrapping his muscular arms around Quin's roommate.

Lou hissed and removed Nero's arm. "It looks like it's going to be twinks against jocks."

"Fine. You all can go to hell," Nero proclaimed. "We'll take you down just as easily," he said putting his arms around Cali and me.

"Do we really have a shot?" I asked Cali.

"Not a chance," he replied.

"Sorry, guys," Nero whispered in our ears.

Once Cage returned and confirmed that Claude would be at the scrimmage, we started the games. Despite losing badly at everything we played, it was still a fun night.

The entire time I wondered why Claude wasn't there. After a few drinks, I asked Cali.

"Claude doesn't come to things like this," he explained.

"We've invited him," Quin volunteered overhearing us. "He never comes."

"Why not?"

Quin shrugged. "I don't know."

"Maybe he can't stand all the damn betrayal," Nero sniped looking at his boyfriend.

Kendall replied, "Sorry, can't hear you over all of the winning."

"You brought this on yourself," Lou added.

"He brought this on all of us," Cage corrected.

"Friendly fire," Quin said looking at his boyfriend longingly.

Watching this group interact, I realized what was missing from my relationship with Jason. He and I didn't have fun together. I sacrificed doing fun things to be with him. It wasn't that he was boring. We just had fun in different ways.

I would love to be a part of a group like this. So, why didn't Claude accept Quin's invitations? Was it because everyone here was into guys and he wasn't?

I know he used to like group hangouts. Back at school, we went to things like this all of the time. I wouldn't have described him as the life of the party, but he spoke more than Cali did tonight.

I missed spending time with Claude. Yeah, there was never a moment when I wasn't attracted to him, but he was also my best friend. We had a lot of fun together. If he were here tonight, I could imagine him joining in on the teasing and then doing his best to hide his ultra-competitive side.

He liked pretending to be chill about everything, but there was a reason he could make up incredible football plays on the fly. He really wanted to win. He just acted like he didn't care. He might have been able to hide that from everyone else, but he couldn't from me.

Hugging everyone and thanking them for the best night I had had in a long time, I continued to think about Claude as we drove back to the bed and breakfast.

"Thanks for inviting, me," I told Cali.

"No problem."

"Do you think Claude will come tomorrow?"

"Maybe."

"You think he's gonna cancel?" I asked Cali not having considered it.

"He always shows up when people need him. But considering Cage told him it was a birthday thing, I wouldn't put it past him."

I thought about the first part of what Cali said. It was true. Claude had always been there when I needed him. It had made falling in love that much harder to resist.

Thinking back on it, was there any way that things couldn't have ended how they had between us? At the time, I was so in love with him that I couldn't see straight. After a night of being around him, I would feel drunk, no alcohol required.

Leaving him to sit in my dorm by myself, I would quickly spiral into sadness. He was a drug that I was addicted to. So after he told me that he would completely cut off my supply, I freaked out. I needed him to breathe, yet, I couldn't have him.

Seeing Claude again was bringing a lot of the old feelings back. Being older and a little wiser, I wasn't going to let myself fall for him like I had before. Yes, I wanted him back in my life. I missed my best friend. But that was all I was looking for.

I didn't want to become addicted to him again. I hated being a junky. And in losing him, I lost myself.

No, I wasn't going back there. Our team needed a quarterback and I needed my best friend.

Having gotten the closest I would get to being forgiven, I wasn't going to ruin things. So even if he were into guys, and by some miracle, me, we couldn't be together. He meant too much to me. I couldn't let it happen.

Chapter 8

Claude

When I received Cage's call, I didn't know what to think. Was he inviting me to his post-birthday hangout because he had seen me jogging near his place? It would be humiliating if it were. As much as I wanted to connect with him, I was still the only Black guy in town. As my mother said, I was the representative for my race for everyone who lived here. I had to act respectably. It was my obligation and duty to my people.

It felt ridiculous even thinking the words, but I've thought a lot about what my mother told me since she said it. I've spent years dissecting and challenging it at its premise. My conclusion has been that it's true.

That meant that my needs came second. I wanted Cage as a friend. At the very least, I desperately needed to feel connected to someone. But I had to do it in a dignified way. Getting a pity invite because he caught me stalking him wasn't dignified.

But whatever the reason I was invited, I was going. I needed this. It was like swimming to the surface for a breath. And I wasn't going to screw this up.

'Am I going to see you on the field?' Titus texted as I got ready to leave.

'You going?' I replied.

'Heading there now. I think Cage is having a quarter-life crisis.'

'Ha!'

'Cali wanted to make sure you were coming?'

'Cali?'

Titus texted a shrug emoji.

Apparently, everyone was going to be there. Having recently seen Cage's brother, Nero, around town, I assumed he would be there too. This was going to be a good way to take my mind off Merri and his offer.

The thing most persuading me to accept Merri's workout was the thought that I could again be part of a team. But maybe I didn't need Merri's help for that. Maybe I could find what I needed here without him.

'I'll see you there,' I texted Titus with building anticipation.

'Do you even remember how to play? Haha!' Titus quipped.

'It's the sport with the round ball and the basket, right?'

He replied with a rolling-on-the-floor-laughing emoji. 'Close enough.'

I wasn't sure why I hadn't told anyone in town about my football past. Could it be that I hadn't taken playing seriously? No, it wasn't that. But perhaps it was because I had taken it too seriously.

Even with the team leaning on me, I had a hard time expressing how much I cared about it. When I was alone, I never watched TV. I studied plays and games I found on YouTube. There were even nights when I couldn't sleep because I kept going over possible plays in my mind.

As much as the way Merri treated me played into my decision to graduate early, I had to admit that it wasn't the only factor. I had been obsessed. I never let it show, but I lived and breathed football. Winning brought elation and losing, spiraling despair.

I didn't tell anyone that was the case because it was too embarrassing. It was just a game. I shouldn't have wanted it so badly. But I did. I never wanted to let down my team. And I definitely didn't want to let down Merri.

Merri had changed my life. He had believed in me before I believed in myself. I liked the way I looked through his eyes.

That was what made how our friendship ended so painful. My mother had made me believe that no one would ever see me past the color of my skin. And for a while, being with Merri made me believe that she was wrong.

Then, when it came down to it, what I feared most was true. In everyone else's eyes, I was just a stereotype, even in the one person I thought I wasn't.

But, he had explained it, hadn't he? He had said what he had because he had been in love with me. I had hurt him by telling him I was leaving. In return, he said things he didn't believe.

Considering that, was it fair to stay mad at him?

Also, if I'm being honest, I'll admit that I told him I was leaving, hoping to hurt him. For weeks before the end, he had been an asshole to me. At one point, not only did he stop texting me, but he also stopped talking to me when we were at the same events.

He even stopped looking me in my eyes. I had missed his kind, steel-gray eyes. Cut off from seeing my reflection in them, I lost a sense of who I was.

He had hurt me. I had hurt him. And then he said something he couldn't take back. That was when I left.

And if I'm still being honest, there was a part of me that thought he was going to chase after me. After all, didn't this all begin because of the way he was treating me? And wasn't he the one who had taken things too far?

Yes, I hadn't made it easy for him to apologize. But was I supposed to? I had cared about him more than anyone I had ever met, and he had crossed a line. He could see that I struggled to trust people, couldn't he? Yet he had betrayed my trust.

Hadn't he realized what he had done? There was a time when I thought that I needed Merri. He had been my source for friends, my source of courage, and my source for feeling good about myself.

But was that true anymore? Without his help, I was finally making a life for myself here. Cage had invited me to hang out without any involvement from Merri. Maybe I didn't need him like I had thought.

So, no longer needing him and with an apology two years too late, where did that leave us? I wasn't sure. I would be lying if I said I hadn't missed my friend. My life hadn't been the same without him.

Before things turned bad between us, we had been inseparable. We talked every day. We ate every meal we could together. And I felt better after seeing him, even if it was just to hear him complain about his girlfriends.

Speaking of that, it's hard to believe he has been gay this entire time. The thought did something to me. I barely knew Merri without a girlfriend. Yet now he was saying it had all been an act? That he had been in love with me from the day we met? Would things between us have been different had I known that back then?

I was certainly never homophobic, but I also wasn't as comfortable with those things as I am now. After all, both of my brothers are involved with men. Titus was dating his best friend, and Cali was with the man he would probably marry.

What if Merri was who I was supposed to be with? Would that be so crazy? He had said he was in love with me. And I had certainly loved him. But did I love him in the same way?

Putting the thought aside, I finished dressing for Cage's scrimmage and drove over. Cage was holding it at my old high school, where he was the coach and P.E. teacher. Pulling up, I found more cars in the parking lot than I had expected. There were almost enough to make me think that there was a game being held.

Getting out and rounding the building, I saw spectators in the bleachers. Spotting Titus, I headed over to him.

"What's going on?" I asked him, getting a questionable look back.

"I didn't know anything about this," he said suspiciously.

"About what?"

"You know that if I knew, I would have told you, right?"

"If you knew what?"

Titus pointed at a guy sitting in the bleachers.

"Merri!" I exclaimed, feeling my heart clench. "What's he doing here?"

"I had nothing to do with this," Titus said, holding up his hands defensively and walking away.

Looking past what had to be the high school football team, I saw Cage. Heading to him, everyone was looking at me like they knew something I didn't.

"Hey, Cage," I said hesitantly. "I thought you mentioned that there would only be a few of us?" I inquired, motioning toward the two dozen people in the stands.

"Yeah, word got out that Nero was going to be here. I guess some people don't have anything better to do on a Saturday," he replied with a smile.

"I guess," I echoed, still unsure what was going on.

"Claude, you son of a bitch!" Nero exclaimed, as he came over and greeted me with a back slap. "How the hell didn't we know?"

"Know what?"

"That all through high school, we were playing with some sort of football genius."

I cringed as soon as he said it. "Merri."

"Hell yeah, Merri," Nero confirmed.

"He told you," I realized, suddenly understanding why Cage had invited me.

It wasn't because of pity or because I was finally building a life for myself here. It had once again been because of Merri. What was my life without him?

"Yeah, he told us," Nero confirmed. "And why did he have to? You won three championships?"

"It's not a big deal."

"There's an NFL scout who's come to this shithole of a town to recruit you? I didn't even get that and I almost went number one in the draft."

"It's not like that. He's a friend. We have history."

"I bet you do," Nero said, looking at Merri. "He's not bad on the eyes, either."

"I didn't mean it like that."

"Uh-huh," he said doubtfully. "Anyway, let's see that amazing arm of yours. You're quarterback for my team. Bro, you're quarterbacking for your kids."

"Look, I haven't played football since…"

"Since winning the Division II national championship. We know. We heard," Nero mocked.

I looked at Merri again.

"How did you guys even meet?"

"Don't you worry about that. Just worry about getting the ball to one of the best running backs in the NFL. You think you can do that?" Nero asked, shoving the ball into my hands with a charismatic grin.

I didn't respond. Instead, I noticed how the ball's leather felt against my skin. I had forgotten the feeling. What had been the point of touching one if Merri hadn't been there to see it?

I again looked at Merri sitting in the bleachers. He was watching me. Turning my attention downfield towards the players huddling around their quarterback, things began to feel familiar.

"Huddle up," I called, as everything slowly came back to me.

Nero, Titus, Cali, and a few of Cage's students joined me. Asking the strangers what positions they played, I set up a formation. Nero was a running back, but I'd use his speed as a wide receiver. Titus and two of the students would be my offensive line. And Cali, who was one of the best university kickers in the nation, I'd use as a floating receiver.

Staring across the line of scrimmage at Cage's team, I saw his students were taking it as seriously as I was. It was likely that Cage had told them that there was an NFL scout watching. That was close enough to being true and would mean they would play like their careers were on the line. Great!

"Down. Set. Hut!" I called.

Grass and bodies flew everywhere. With Titus in front of me, I found the pocket. With my eyes bouncing between Cali and Nero, I waited until Nero had shaken his defender and launched the ball. Everyone stopped to watch. With Nero's speed, it had to travel forty yards before finally hitting him in the hands.

"Touchdown!" Nero yelled, dancing in the end zone.

I turned to find Merri. He had stood to watch the pass. With Nero performing the most atrocious celebration dance I had ever seen, Merri looked at me and smiled. Something within me lit up. For the first time in years, I felt alive.

Switching to defense, Titus took the lead. Directing us where we needed to go, we got into position and fought as Cage's well-organized offensive line held us back. As if performing a tit-for-tat, Cage's wide receiver broke free of Nero's defensive coverage and scored a touchdown.

"Stay on him," I yelled.

"Not my job," Nero yelled back.

"Stay on him!" I insisted, knowing that Cage was out to prove he was still as good as he had been.

That was when the real fun began. Locked into a one-on-one battle with Cage, I turned to Titus.

"I want you to defend, slip your man, spin, receive, and run. Got it?"

"Got it."

"Repeat it back."

"Defend, slip, spin, receive, and run," he confirmed.

I was impressed. These weren't instructions offensive linemen often received.

"And then you'll fake the pass to him and find me, right?" Nero asked.

I pointed at him. "Decoy."

"You're kidding?" Nero challenged.

"Decoy! Repeat it back."

Nero sighed. "Decoy."

"Break," I ordered, sending everyone to their positions.

"Hut," I yelled before watching the play unfold.

Titus defended, overpowered his man, ran, spun, and waited. It had been close enough. Because with Cage sending both deep defenders after Nero, Titus was wide open. Hitting him with a bullet pass, he locked his hands around the ball and chugged his way to the end zone.

"Touchdown!" Nero yelled as Titus collapsed desperately out of breath.

Cage and I met gazes. He was impressed, having not seen the play coming. That was when he dug in, drawing up plays like it was a championship game.

Using all four downs and our weak defense, Cage eventually scored. But I had just begun. Designing a play for Cali to score, we set it up and ran it.

"Touchdown! Did you see that, bro? Every person on our team is gonna score on you, and there's nothing you can do to stop it," Nero said riding a high.

Although I hadn't said it, Nero had figured out my plan. I was going to design a play for each of my players so that they all got a chance to score. Nero hadn't made it any easier by announcing it to their defenders, but harder was better.

With the four high school students looking at me nervously, I showed them my clenched fist. Turning to the first of them, I asked,

"Have you ever scored in a game before?"

"I play defensive line and warm the bench," he said practically shaking.

"If you run, can you make it to the end zone?"

Without a word, he took off running. I had to call him back.

Nero snickered. "Good thing they won't know who you're going to throw to next."

"They won't if you're the quarterback. Do you know how to do a handoff?"

Lining up on the line of scrimmage to the left of Titus, everyone on Cage's team looked at me, confused.

"Down, set, hut," Nero shouted before they knew what was happening.

Curling behind him, I took the ball and ran. Still not knowing what was going on, the defense collapsed towards me. Dragging them to the other side of the field, I yelled, "Hey!"

It was enough to get my benched defensive lineman to turn around. Firing the ball cross-field, I hit him in the hands. I thought it was too hard, but he held onto it. The look on his face was delightful. I had never seen someone beam with more joy.

"Touchdown!" Nero yelled, running over and grabbing me around the neck.

The last of the high schoolers wasn't as easy. For him, we ran plays that inched us up the field five yards at a time. Now committed to the idea, a yard away from the end zone, we all blocked as the last of our players scored his touchdown.

My team screamed in victory. I couldn't imagine them having more fun than they had today. I enjoyed it, too, though I didn't show it. It was enough to know I had made it happen. And they were having a great time without me.

"Bro, it looks like he is better than you," Nero taunted Cage. "Where was all of this when we needed it in high school?" he asked me.

"We had a quarterback," I reminded him.

He gave me a look that was more annoyed than amused.

As Merri stepped up, Nero turned to him and said, "I guess you weren't lying."

"I was not," Merri said, beaming.

Having Merri so close to me made me feel warm. I desperately wanted to ask if he had seen me. I didn't, knowing he had.

"No, seriously, Claude," Titus interjected, looking shell-shocked. "Why didn't you ever try out for quarterback in high school?"

I looked at him and then at Nero and Merri.

"I guess I didn't want to make waves."

"So, you just let someone who isn't as good as you have what you deserved?" Titus challenged.

"You say that like it would have been the first time. My life has been about dancing that line between being good enough and being too good. When you look like me, people can't see you as a threat. Things can get dangerous," I said with a forced smile.

"And by 'look like you,' you mean because you're black," Titus asked directly.

I looked around, not needing to acknowledge the truth of it.

"Shit!" Cali exclaimed. "That fuckin' sucks."

"You get used to it," I said, downplaying how much it weighed on me.

"You shouldn't have to," Cali said angrily.

"Thanks," I took a deep breath. "Do you mind if I head out?"

All the guys looked at each other.

Cage, who had joined us, responded, "Quin and the others are setting up an open bar at our place. We were hoping you would join us."

"I'm actually pretty tired. It's been a while since I've played. I'm not in the same shape as I used to be."

"Oh, okay," Cage said, disappointed. "If you change your mind, you know where we are."

"Of course," I said with a smile.

When everyone but Merri had left, he asked, "Are you sure you don't want to join them? Cali invited me to game night last night. It was a good time. They're a great group of guys."

"You can go if you want," I told him, unsure how he had met them.

"No, I was just thinking you might want to."

"I'm good," I told him, already feeling far more exposed than I felt comfortable.

"Where are you going?" Merri asked me.

"Not sure yet."

Merri looked at me nervously. "Do you mind if I hang with you?"

I thought about it. As much as I wanted him to, I wondered if I should let him.

"That's fine," I said, walking to my car.

"I didn't drive, so…"

"Where are you staying?"

"Cali's bed and breakfast."

"That's how you ended up at game night," I realized.

"I asked him to show me the town's nightlife."

I laughed. "I'm sorry about that."

"Don't be. Free drinks, hot guys, and if you count what Quin did on our game board corpses, there was dancing. A night can't get any better than that?"

I laughed. "Well, is there any other part of the town you'd like to see while you're here?"

Merri smiled.

"I saw on a website that this area has more waterfalls than any other part of the country."

"Yes. I've read that somewhere," I said, amused that he was quoting my tour company's website back to me.

"Well, I haven't made reservations, but it would sure be nice to see some of them."

"You want a pre-season tour?" I clarified.

"I mean, I don't want to come across as a big shot, but I do know one of the owners. I might be able to convince him to let us."

"I hope you know the friendly one. Because the other can be a real asshole."

Merri gazed into my eyes.

"Oh, I don't know. I think the other one is pretty nice, too. You should try being nicer to him. At least, that's what I'm doing," he said with a vulnerable smile.

My chest clenched hearing his words. Merri was trying to get us to start over. I didn't hate that idea. And picturing him back in my life felt good.

"Huh! Let me know how that turns out," I said, holding back everything I wanted to say.

Heading to the office, I parked and walked Merri to the storage area behind the main cabin.

"Titus is the one who usually gives the tours."

"So, you're the brains and he's the brawn," he said flirtatiously.

"You could say that," I replied, as my body reacted to his suggestion. "How do you feel about getting wet?"

"You don't know how long I've been waiting for you to ask me that," he said with a smile.

I laughed.

"Be careful what you wish for," I cautioned him.

"Why? Are you gonna make me regret it?"

"I might," I told him, feeling the electricity crackle between us.

"I'd like to see that," Merri said, placing his body inches in front of mine.

Feeling the heat pulse between us, I stepped back. "You win."

This was a game we used to play. Back then, it was between two straight friends. At least I thought it had been. He had always been willing to take it a step further than I was. Now knowing that he was gay, I understood why.

But that was then. The question was, why would I initiate the game now? Not only had he confirmed he was gay, but he had said that he had been in love with me.

I wasn't cruel. I didn't play with people's emotions. So, why had I flirted back?

Unable to put the question aside, Merri helped me retrieve one of the canoes and together we carried it to the nearby river.

"This is amazing!" Merri proclaimed as he marveled at the scene in front of us.

"Do you understand why I came back?" I asked with a smile.

Merri tried to respond convincingly but couldn't. "Yeah, I get it now."

It was obvious that he didn't. At least not from the scenery. And that made sense because it wasn't true. I had run home because of him. He had hurt me, and I couldn't deal with it.

As much as I had liked the way I looked through Merri's eyes, I also knew that he had never really seen me. I was sure of it because I had never let him. I didn't let anyone.

What would happen if I did? What if, for once, I allowed someone in? What would that do to me? How would that change things?

"You weren't kidding about getting wet," Merri said after I explained to him how we would get into the canoe.

"There was a time I couldn't keep you out of the water. Do you remember when you went swimming with inches of snow on the ground?" I reminded him.

"It was at Big Bear. I regret it to this day. It's a miracle I still have all of my toes."

I laughed.

"Well, the river isn't that cold," I told him as I took off my shoes and socks, stepped into the water, and held the canoe.

"I'm getting flashbacks," he said, doing the same and following me in.

With minimal splash, we both got in and grabbed a paddle.

"It feels like we're paddling down the Amazon or something."

"Similar. But fewer anacondas hanging from trees."

"You all have snakes hanging from trees here?" Merri said, searching the canopy of branches shading us.

I laughed.

"Where's the outdoorsman who would drag me to one campsite after another?" I asked the guy sitting with his back to me.

"Okay. Confession. I just took you to them because I wanted to get you alone. I hate camping. Hate it!"

"No, you don't," I said, not believing him for a second.

"I do. If I ever have to poop in another hole I've dug, it will be too soon," he said, not taking his eyes off the trees.

"No. What you hate is pooping in the woods. Or, forgetting your sleeping pad and having to sleep on the ground."

"Oh, you still think I accidentally forgot my sleeping pad?"

"What do you mean?"

"What always happened after I told you I had forgotten it?" he asked me.

I thought back.

"You complained about it."

Merri chuckled.

"After that."

"It was endless. You never stopped complaining," I said sincerely.

"I did, after you invited me to share yours."

I paused.

"So, you intentionally forgot your sleeping pad to sleep on mine."

"The dream was to get into your sleeping bag, but you were clearly not having that."

"I thought you were joking when you suggested it," I said, vividly remembering the incidents.

Merri shrugged, gave up his search for snakes, and then paddled.

"So, every camping trip we took was just you trying to get into my sleeping bag?"

Merri relented. "Maybe not every trip. But it was on my mind."

"Wow!"

"Yeah, I was kind of an asshole back then," Merri decided.

I stared at the back of his head.

"But you're not anymore?"

"It depends on who you talk to. My ex might have an opinion on that. You two might see eye to eye."

"I don't think you were an asshole," I admitted.

"I was. Especially to you," he said, looking back.

"You had your moments. Or, specifically, one moment. But otherwise, you were the best friend I ever had."

"Until I screwed it up," he said, looking away.

"Until you screwed it up," I agreed. "But, mistakes happen."

He looked back again.

"That's very kind of you. And, maybe one day you'll forgive me?"

"Let's not push it," I joked.

"Right," he said, looking away, embarrassed.

"I'm kidding. What happened to your sense of humor?"

Merri turned his body fully facing me.

"I'm just really sorry about what I said. You don't know how much I've thought about it. I know you didn't ask for me to feel about you the way I did, but I felt it. I was so in love with you. You don't know how much.

"You would be the last thing I thought about before I fell asleep and the first thing I thought about when I woke up. Knowing I would see you made my day. And, when I didn't, or you had to cancel, my world fell apart."

"Merri, I had no idea."

"How could you? I didn't tell you. I could barely admit it to myself. All I knew was that the sun rose and set around you. And then, because I couldn't keep it in my pants, I fucked it all up."

"I was fucked up way before you said what you did," I told him sincerely.

"Are you kidding? You were the most together person I knew. I wanted to be you."

"You shouldn't have. Do you know that I didn't even tell my brothers that I played football?"

Merri looked away in thought.

"Yeah, what was up with that? I mentioned that you won us championships, and no one had heard a word about it. How could you not tell anyone? Everyone from my elementary school knew we had won that first year, and all I was was the waterboy."

"And masseuse."

"I was your masseuse. If you hadn't blabbed about it, I would never have offered to rub other football players' feet."

I laughed. "Sorry about that."

"No, you're not," he said with a smile. "But seriously, why didn't you tell anybody?"

I stopped paddling and looked down.

"I have a hard time letting people in."

"Why?"

"Because if people know too much about you, they can use it to hurt you."

Merri remained silent.

"Before meeting you, I had a hard time trusting anyone."

"And then I broke your trust," he said, saying something I couldn't deny. Merri moved closer to me. When he was kneeling inches in front of me, he said, "I'm really sorry, Claude. I truly and sincerely am. I was just so in love with you. I…"

And that was when I kissed him.

[*Reading Companion Suggestion: Did you enjoy that? Know someone who would enjoy it too? Share this book with them now because you're going to want to chat with them about it as soon as you're done. J*]

Chapter 9

Merri

Claude's lips were on mine. How were Claude's lips on mine? How many times had I dreamed of this? How many times had I pleasured myself to this thought?

The sensation was everything I thought it would be. His full, firm lips were warm and soft. Heat flashed through my body. I felt light-headed.

As I saw his hand moving toward me, presumably to clutch the back of my neck, I pulled away. I don't know why, but I did. Staring into his surprised eyes, I couldn't speak.

"Sorry," he said quickly, looking away, painted with embarrassment.

"Oh! Ahh! No worries, mate!" I replied more awkwardly than I'd replied to anything in my life.

No worries, mate? Did I actually say that? Did kissing him turn me Australian? What the hell was I doing?

Turning around as if nothing had happened, I grabbed my paddle. Shell-shocked, I paddled forward. Claude said nothing. Nor did I. It was possible my brain had short-circuited.

As I mentally listed the symptoms of a stroke, Claude broke the silence.

"This river isn't actually part of the tour. Like I said, my brother usually does them."

"Yeah, I meant to ask you about that," I said, finding a safe off-ramp from whatever had just happened. "You have brothers… who don't exactly look like you?"

"You don't think so?"

I looked back, wondering if he was joking. He wasn't.

"I mean, you all have those dimples, but I could say the same thing about Cage and Nero. Is everyone here related?"

"Not as far as I know."

"Then, you don't look that much alike."

"Huh," Claude huffed.

"And there's that other thing?" I brought up gently.

"What other thing?"

"You know, the thing that makes you look different from Titus and Cali."

"Do you mean that I'm black and they aren't?"

I turned around, looking surprised. "Wait, you're black? Wow! I guess I just don't see color."

"Is this new?" Claude joked.

"Actually, yeah. It's a new policy. And it makes it a hell of a time getting dressed."

Claude laughed.

"But since you brought it up, what's with that?"

"We share a biological father. Titus's boyfriend was handing out DNA tests looking for Titus's birth father and found Cali and me instead."

"Do you know who your father is?"

"We have a name, but it doesn't come up on any searches."

"Have you asked your mother about him?"

"She's who gave us the name. Titus and Cali's moms wouldn't say anything about him."

"Are you curious?"

As I looked back, Claude shrugged.

"It would be good to know for health reasons. But considering how little our mothers want to talk about him, it might be better not knowing."

"Do you think he might have been a football player?"

"You mean because Titus, Cali, and I all play?"

"Yeah. And don't Titus and Cali also hold conference records?"

"They do."

"Then unless all of your mothers are ridiculously athletic, his seed couldn't have fallen far from the tree."

"I guess. But I get the feeling there's something else. Something that we wouldn't want to know."

"Interesting." I gave it a moment and then said, "Speaking of interesting things. Have you given any thought to the workout with the Cougars?"

"On the field today, I was thinking about it a lot."

"And?" I asked, feeling a chill of anticipation rattle through me.

"It's been two years," he admitted.

"I told you, I can train you like I used to in the off-season."

"I don't know."

"It's just a workout. It's not like you have your whole life resting on it like other people do. If, somehow, things don't happen the way I think they will, you can return to your life here. You can get back to giving the lamest tours in the history of man."

"You think my tour is lame?" Claude asked, feigning being offended.

"Hell, yes. Have you told me what that plant is called?" I asked, gesturing to a bush on the edge of the river. "No, you haven't. Have you pointed out any snakes in the trees? Not a one. You started it off promising danger and excitement. Since?" I faked a yawn.

"You're bored, huh?"

"A little," I replied contentiously.

"Did I tell you that the snakes around here swim?"

"They what?" I asked, feeling my heart jump into my throat.

"They swim. In rivers like this. In fact, isn't that one there?"

"Where?" I asked, whipping around.

"Oh no!" Claude said suddenly rocking the boat violently.

"Don't you…"

"Oh no!" Claude repeated before grabbing both sides of the canoe and flipping us over.

The cold, snake-infested water soaked through my clothes, scalding my skin. I could feel the length of an imaginary anaconda wrap around me, trying to swallow me whole.

"Ahhh!" I screamed, forgetting how to swim.

When something touched the bottom of my foot, my head nearly exploded. It turned out to be the ground. The river wasn't that deep. But it didn't matter.

Swimming like my life depended on it, I shot to the edge of the river. Dragging myself ashore, I rolled until there was a distance between me and the site of my doom.

"Not funny!" I yelled at Claude.

He couldn't hear me over his laughter.

"That's it, you fuckin' owe me. We're doin' a workout. You're gonna be at today's football field at 9 AM tomorrow morning, and you are gonna run until you can't walk. I mean it."

"Okay, okay. Whatever. I'll be there," he said, composing himself.

"Oh, you said that like you still had a choice," I said, legitimately annoyed.

"Did I tell you how often snakes sleep in the dirt next to the shore?"

"Ahhh!" I screamed, racing to my feet, brushing off whatever was on me.

Claude, again, rolled in laughter.

"Not... funny!"

Once Claude regained his composure, he was eventually able to get me back in the boat. I couldn't stay mad at him. After all, seeing him laugh so completely had warmed my heart.

It had been a long time since I had seen him laugh like that. It had to have been before I snapped and things went south. Remembering that, I decided that I would pretend our kiss didn't happen.

As far as I knew, Claude was, and had always been, straight. He'd never expressed an interest in me or any guy. I'm sure because I've watched him. His eyes didn't light up when he saw me, like I knew mine did when I saw him. No one ignited his fire.

Knowing that, to go down that path with him would be dangerous. I had lost my mind the last time I had allowed myself to feel something for him. So whatever experimentation he was looking to do with me was not welcome. I wanted a professional and personal relationship with him. That's all. Nothing intimate.

Ending the tour and carrying the canoe back, I pointed out how we had only seen one waterfall.

"I'm just saying that it wasn't what was promised on the website. 'The most waterfalls in the country.' That's what it said."

"You want the full tour? Buy a ticket," Claude insisted.

"You just better hope I don't leave a review. And if you're expecting a tip, good luck with that," I said, teasing him.

On the drive to my bed and breakfast, for the first time in years, I felt like I had my best friend back. We talked. At first, it was about my last year at university. Later, the conversation turned to how it was working as Papa's assistant.

"Have you two been getting along?" he asked, referring to the stories I had told him back at school.

"Sure. He's been pretty good about things since I came out. It was like he finally let go of who he wanted me to be and accepted me for who I am."

"Is that good?"

"It's better than the alternative, which is me feeling his disappointment every time I entered a room."

"I don't know what he could ever feel disappointed about."

"Thanks. But I always got the feeling that if he had to choose between the two of us, he would have chosen you as a son."

"I doubt that."

"That's because you and him are so similar. Neither of you ever expresses what you're feeling to the people you care about. The way he used to talk about you when you weren't around, there was no way I could compare. 'Claude gets straight A's and has led our team to multiple championships. I can't even get you to put your dishes in the sink,'" I said, imitating Papa.

"Sorry about that," Claude offered.

"About what?" I imitated my father again. "About being so goddamn perfect? About being the finest specimen ever put on a football field?" I paused. "You know, a part of me thinks he sent me here just so he could have his prodigal son back."

"Your father sent you here?" Claude asked, surprised.

"Partially."

"Huh," Claude huffed, bringing an end to his questions.

Remaining silent for the final minute of our drive, when we parked at the bed and breakfast, I placed my hand on the door handle.

"So, will I see you tomorrow?" I asked him, feeling as nervous as I had the first day I met him.

"I'll be there," he said with a smile.

God, how I liked to see him smile. It was almost as much as I liked kissing him. Too bad I could never let that happen again.

"Good. Be prepared to work," I told him before leaving him behind and heading for my room.

Changing out of my still damp clothes, I lay in bed, wondering what I should do next. I considered replying to Papa's texts. The problem with that was I didn't know what to tell him.

Claude hadn't yet agreed to workout for the Cougars. So far, he was only letting me warm him up. But if that went well, maybe then?

After coming up with a schedule for tomorrow's warmup, I drove to the local diner, watching as a handful of people streamed in and out. I considered what it might be like to live here. Hanging out with Cali and the others had been more fun than I had had in years. If Claude didn't make the team and he asked me to, could I move here?

Getting to bed early, I called Claude the next day just to be sure he was still coming.

"Hey Merri, what's up?" he asked, offering me the greeting he had for years.

"You there yet?"

"Merri, it's 8:15."

"You know what coach says," I reminded him.

"If you're on time, you're late?"

"Exactly."

"And when have I ever been late?"

"Two years is a long time. Things change."

"If I remember correctly, he came up with that saying because of you. So, are you there yet?"

"I might have been in an unhealthy, long-term relationship with 'showing up on time' back then. But, like I said, in two years, things change."

"I better not show up before you."

"Impossible. I'm walking out the door right now," I said, rolling over in bed.

"You're walking out the door now?"

"That's what I said."

"What color's the door?"

"What?" I said, sitting up.

"You heard me. If you're walking out the door now, tell me the color of the door."

"What are you, testing me?" I said, scrambling to my feet and finding my pants.

"You stalling me?"

Dressing, I said, "No, I'm just deeply offended that you would doubt me like that."

"I'm still not hearing the color," Claude pointed out.

"That's because I'm processing what it says that you think so little of me that you would ask that question," I said, hurrying from my room to the stairs.

"You're still not saying."

"That's because... brown," I blurted out as soon as it was in sight. "And it has a teardrop-shaped stained glass in the center of it."

I sat on the stairs silently catching my breath.

"Okay. Tell Cali I said hi."

"What?"

I looked down the stairs toward the kitchen and spotted Cali texting on his phone. He looked up at me.

"Claude says hello," I told him.

"Thanks."

"Is that who you're texting with?" I asked Cali.

"Have been all morning," Cali pointed out. "Breakfast?" He asked, returning to the kitchen.

"I was awake," I told Claude.

"Yes. You were the one who called me. I was very impressed. There was a time when you struggled to get up by 11."

"Well, I have a job now," I clarified.

"You had a job then."

"Coach understood. He was fine with it."

"Was he?"

Claude was right. My father never was.

"Just be on time, okay," I told him.

"If you're on time, you're late," he told me, having successfully frustrated my morning.

"Bye, Claude."

Ending the call, I continued to sit on the stairs. I couldn't help but smile. It felt like old times. I had missed this so much. How would it feel when we both returned to our lives?

As much as my father wanted Claude back, Claude hadn't been wrong about things. As sharp as Claude had been yesterday, he wasn't at an NFL level. That didn't mean he couldn't get there. But he looked a step slow.

Papa wanted to see him as quickly as I could get him there. Papa said that he would know if he was still the same man if he could see him on the field. What neither of us had expected was that he wouldn't pick up a football in two years. That's a long time to be away from a sport that rewards daily improvements.

Putting this out of my mind, I got up and headed to the kitchen. Along with Cali, I found a selection of cereals, fruits, and pastries.

"We have pancakes, scrambled eggs, and sausages. Any interest?" Cali asked.

"It all sounds good," I admitted.

"Then give me a few minutes."

"Got it." I was about to head back up to my room to get ready when I paused. "Did you know Claude in high school?"

"He was a few years ahead of me, but yea, I knew him by sight. He was the only black kid in our school."

"Do you know if he had a hard time growing up?"

Cali shook his head unsure. "As far as I know, everyone liked him. Why?"

"I guess I'm still trying to piece together why no one knew he played football at university."

"I'm trying to figure that out, too."

"Has he ever given you any advice about football?"

"He's never brought it up."

"Has he ever gone to one of your games?"

"Not that I know of."

I thought about that.

"I couldn't imagine doing the things he did and not mentioning it to anyone?"

"I thought I was getting to know him," Cali admitted, looking saddened.

Staring at him, I could tell that he was genuinely hurt that Claude hadn't told him.

"But I'm sure you know other things, right? You guys must talk pretty often."

"We talk," he said, not looking at me.

"Then maybe it's just that topic that he doesn't like to discuss."

"Something tells me that it's not just that."

"What do you mean?"

"When you pull on a thread, right?" He asked, looking for confirmation.

"How lonely must he be?" I asked, wondering if what I had done had caused this.

Cali mixed ingredients instead of responding.

"Anyway, I'll be back down in a few. I can't be late."

"You're late!" Claude pointed out as I jogged onto the field.

"Traffic," I suggested.

"Really?" Claude asked, surprised.

"Yeah. I passed another car on the way here and…" I made the gesture of my head exploding.

"It confused you?"

"I wasn't sure what to do with myself."

"I see," Claude said, amused. "By the way, did you ask permission for us to be here?"

I looked around at the empty school building and parking lot.

"Did I have to?" I asked sincerely.

Claude laughed sarcastically and, then took out his phone.

"I'll let Cage know we're here."

"See, this is the type of partnership we could have. Yin and Yang," I said, gesturing between us. "I'm the ideas person and you're the execution."

Ignoring me, he read from his phone, "He said we're fine to use it."

"Great! Have you warmed up?"

Claude opened his mouth, searching for a reply.

"Stretch and give me a lap," I said, indicating the circumference of the field.

Without a word, Claude went to work. When that was done, I took him through some of the things he would need to do in the workout. Despite taking two years off, he wasn't bad.

His sprint times were still good for a quarterback. And his ability to change direction, although not what it used to be, wasn't far off.

"Did you do any sports at all these last two years?"

"Depends. Do you consider getting coffee a sport?"

"Was it at Starbucks during rush hour?"

"It was on the back deck of your bed and breakfast."

I stared at him with a 'don't be ridiculous' look.

"Well, for a guy who has given up on life, you're not that out of shape."

"I haven't given up on life."

"Have you lifted anything heavier than a fork in the last two years?"

"I carried all of our touring equipment to our new office."

I stared at him again. Looking away, I said, "I'll take that as a no."

It was Claude's turn to be annoyed. That was okay because Claude always performed better when he had something to prove. And when, after a series of wind sprints, he was dripping with sweat, he whipped off his shirt.

God damn! He had been lifting something heavier than a fork. Because that man was ripped. Somehow he now had a better body than when he was the starting quarterback for a Division II championship team.

Getting aroused as I stared at him, I looked away. That helped downstairs, but my fair skin was no match for how I was feeling. Turning back around, I was glowing. Claude laughed… that bastard.

"How did your people ever end up stealing all that land?" Claude had once asked me. "Everything you think is written on your face," he teased, having watched me turn shades of red. "No, seriously, how?"

"We can't all have a perfect complexion like you," I had replied, hinting at my true feelings for him.

"I wouldn't say perfect," he said, feigning cockiness.

Although I knew Claude had just been giving me a hard time, he had hit a sore spot. I envied Claude's beautifully brown skin. If I could cut it off him and wear it, I would. I mean, I wouldn't. But the man's complexion was just so smooth and beautiful, while I was like a mood ring I was so pale. It was fuckin' unfair!

"Rest up and do the sprints again," I ordered, before heading to the bleachers.

Doing as I said, Claude collected his breath for another few minutes, and then ran again. It never took much to get Claude to work hard. He had always been ready to run until he collapsed.

Watching his strong body sprint from one yard line to another, I wondered if I was doing the right thing by having him workout for the team. He had yet to say whether he wanted this. I wasn't even sure if he still liked football, or if he ever had.

He had to like some parts of it. No one got to be as good as he was without putting in hours that no one else saw. But why was he letting me put him through this now?

"What's next?" Claude asked when he walked over, fighting for breath.

"Next is that you tell me that you want to workout for the Cougars," I said stoically.

"What do you mean?"

"I mean, I want you to tell me that it's something you want to do."

"I'm here, doing these wind sprints, aren't I?"

"Yeah, but do you want to be?"

He looked at me annoyed. "If we're done, then let me know. I'll head home."

"If we're done? No. What do you mean?" I asked, confused.

"I mean, you came here, made me some grand offer, told me how much you had been in love with me, and now you're asking me if I wanna be here?"

I squinted and shook my head, trying to understand what was happening.

"I don't know what to say to that. Yes, that's what happened."

He looked at me, frustrated. "Then I'm done."

"Whoa! Where did that come from?"

"I kissed you!" he shouted, charging towards me.

"Oh! Yeah," I said, looking away.

"Yeah!"

Cringing, I asked, "Can we pretend like you didn't?"

Claude stared at me with his mouth hanging open before resigning.

"Yeah. Fuck it. Whatever."

Seeing how upset he was, I tried to explain.

"I'm actually trying to be good. I'm trying to do the right thing here."

"By pretending it didn't happen?"

"Isn't that what you do?" I asked, referring to him not telling any of his friends about the part of his life that involved me.

Claude's anger deflated to resignation.

"Whatever," he told me, no longer going anywhere.

"Look," I said, gathering my words. "I just want you to do this for the right reasons. You gave up football pretty easily. If you do the workout, I want you to do it because you want to be there, not because I want you to.

"I mean, there's a part of me screaming that I should take what I can get when it comes to you. But we know how that turned out last time. So, I just wanna know, is the workout something you want?"

Claude rocked onto his heels, giving it sincere thought. After a moment, he said, "If someone had asked me that a week ago, I would have said it wasn't. But you being here reminded me of the things I loved. And I was born to play football.

"When I'm in a pocket with the ball in my hand, I feel alive. Nothing else matters. I miss that. And if you're telling me I could have that again, I want it."

A smile arose from deep inside of me.

"Then, let's get it."

"You think I'm ready?" Claude asked doubtfully.

"I think you're gonna be one of the greatest quarterbacks in the history of the NFL. And I think they'll see it."

"But it feels so quick."

"Papa asked to see you as soon as possible."

"And you think I won't embarrass myself?"

"Claude, you couldn't embarrass yourself if you tried. So, what do you say? Are you ready to do this?"

Claude looked away in thought.

Seeing his hesitation, I said, "Come on, Claude, say you're ready to do this."

"I'm ready," he replied meekly.

I smiled. "I need to hear it louder than that. I said, are you ready?"

"I'm ready," he said a little louder.

"I said, are you ready?" I yelled.

"I'm ready," he shouted with a smile.

"Then let's do this!" I said, grabbing his shoulders and shaking him excitedly.

With Claude on board, we ran passing drills until his arm tired, and then we each headed home. It was as I packed that it hit me. Everything I ever wanted was now at stake. The team's owner had wanted me to quit. When I didn't, he started looking for any excuse to fire me.

If I brought in Claude and he didn't do well, not only could it be the excuse the owner wanted, but Claude could decide he was done with me. He could get upset because I got him to trust me and then let him down again.

If things didn't go well, I could lose everything. And more important than that, I could lose Claude.

With my skin tingling like it was on fire, I prepared to check out. Expensing a round-trip plane ticket for Claude, I thought about what it meant. I had three days to convince him not to disappear from my life again. How was I going to do that?

Claude, who never shared anything personal, had shared that he had a problem trusting people. Well, somehow I had gotten him to trust me again. But if things didn't work out like I had convinced him they would, would I have broken his trust? Would this time be the final straw? Would I lose him forever?

My heart pounded painfully as I packed. Not being able to relax, I didn't get any sleep. Dragging myself out of bed in the morning, I was exhausted. And picking up Claude to drive us to the airport, I felt like I was losing my mind.

Because I couldn't focus on anything, I was sensitive to everything. Like how he didn't invite me in to meet the one person in his life he had told me about. During three years of university together, I hadn't met his mother. It had made me think that he was hiding her from me. But, in reality, was he hiding me from her?

Pushing that out of my mind as we drove to the airport, I managed not to say anything crazy until we were on the plane. With the doors locked and our trip inevitable, my insecurities got the better of me.

"I just want to point out that we aren't going to Miami," I told him as our plane approached the runway.

"I know," he replied casually.

As we approached our destination, I said,

"Our team is based in the Panhandle. There's not going to be anything fancy around."

Claude looked at me amused.

"You just saw where I'm from. I think I'm okay with 'nothing fancy.'"

"Pensacola's a little different than your town?"

"How so?"

I considered how unfriendly the city was to gay people. It didn't make the place much fun for me to live in. But would that affect Claude?

Yeah, he had kissed me. But what did that mean? It wasn't like he was into me, right? And even if, by some miracle, he was into me, I couldn't let my mind go there. I couldn't handle being wrong about that too.

"It's Florida. You've heard of the Florida Man, right?"

Claude swept his hand in front of him like a newspaper headline.

"You mean like, 'Florida man robs gas station with alligator'?"

"Right."

"Or, 'Florida man throws alligator through Wendy's drive-thru window'?"

"Yeah."

"Or, 'Florida man gets eaten alive while attempting to rob a gas station at a Wendy's drive-thru with an alligator'?"

"You're familiar with it," I confirmed. "Now imagine those people wearing their shirt while they do those things, and that's Pensacola."

"Got it. And I assume they're also not a fan of black people."

"Oh, that part's a given," I said, attempting to be funny.

"Got it," Claude said, not finding it as humorous as I had hoped.

"Honestly, I don't know how they treat black people there. It's probably as bad as anywhere else. There are good and bad people everywhere, right?"

"Yeah. That's what I figured," Claude said, withdrawing a little.

I looked out the plane's window trying to recover from being an insensitive prick.

"How bad was it being black in Oregon?" I asked, turning back to him.

Claude thought about it.

"It could have been worse. It helps that we were in a university town. But I try not to look for the things I don't want to see."

"So, things were cool there?"

"I mean, I did get a few people asking to touch my hair."

"Seriously?" I asked, cringing.

"There were a few."

"I'm sorry about that," I said, apologizing for all white people everywhere.

"Listen, if that was the worst thing that happened to me while I was there, I would have been fine with it," he said with a sarcastic smile.

"What was the worst thing?" I asked, nervously.

He just stared at me.

"Fuck!" I said, realizing that what I had said had been it. "I'm so sorry, man."

"I get it."

"It's just that, in all of the time I knew you, I really wanted to touch your hair. I didn't know how to ask…" I shrugged longingly.

Claude looked at me for a moment and then burst into laughter.

"Can I do it now?" I said, reaching for him.

"Get off me," he said, pulling away.

"Claude, can I touch your hair?" I teased.

"Get off!" He said, giving me a push.

I settled, feigning disappointment. "This will not help race relations," I joked.

"You're an idiot."

I pointed at myself. "Florida Man."

Claude laughed.

Hearing Claude laugh made me feel better. It always did. It had a magical ability to make me believe that everything would be okay.

Landing in Pensacola, I immediately texted Papa letting him know Claude had agreed to do the workout. I had waited until now, fearing Claude would change his mind. I knew I might have, considering what had happened between us. But with the plane on the ground and him in Pensacola, I finally felt free to set things in motion.

"Coach says he's setting things up. He has to coordinate with the general manager and a few others. He'll let me know when he has the day and time."

"What do we do until then? Did you get me a hotel room?"

My panic-sensitive brain lit up.

"Shit! Did you want one?" I asked sincerely. "I was thinking you would stay with me. On the couch, I mean. Is that fine? I swear it's comfortable. Or, I could take the couch."

Claude stared at me.

"No, I can sleep on the couch."

I could tell what he was thinking.

"If you want a hotel room, I can get you one. I just figured that there's not much to do in Pensacola and you'd prefer to stay with me. My place isn't big or fancy, but at least you would know someone."

"It's okay. Your place is fine," he said with a kind smile.

It was only as I looked into his warm eyes that I actually thought about my place. I had been so focused on getting him here that I hadn't put any thought into what he would be expecting.

Driving back to my place, I held my breath.

"It isn't much," I said as I let him in.

He scanned my one-bedroom, apartment, not saying anything.

"What I learned when I got the job was that assistant coaches don't make a lot," I admitted.

It wasn't that my apartment was bad or messy. It was just small and still unfurnished. It had the necessities—a comfortable couch, a 60-inch TV, and a PlayStation. But when it came to the things that made my apartment look like a gay guy lived there, it was lacking.

Claude sat on the couch.

"Comfortable," he confirmed, patting the gray cushions.

"It's also pretty wide. I've slept on it a lot. When I do, I sleep through the night. It's not bad."

"Cool," he said mutedly.

I looked around my space for the first time with fresh eyes. It really was pretty drab. My ex had referred to it as my dorm room. More specifically, he said that it looked like a child lived here. And I would have taken offense to that if I hadn't been eating cereal over the sink with a plastic fork when he said it.

"I haven't gotten the chance to finish furnishing it yet."

"How long have you been living here?"

"About a year," I admitted. "But you know how it is during football season. I'm on the road half of the time. Then, when I'm here, all I want to do is fall asleep on the couch playing PlayStation."

"I guess some things never change," he said with a smile.

"I guess not," I said, relaxing.

Putting down his travel bag, we headed back out to get something to eat. This was going to be my first chance to convince him not to leave me forever. I had to choose precisely the right place.

"Is this a Tennessee-themed bar?" Claude asked, scanning the decorations lining the walls.

"Bluegrass Bourbons," I said proudly. "It's a whiskey bar. Doesn't it make you feel at home?"

Claude looked around at everything from the vanity license plate that read 'TN2STEP' to the miniaturized whiskey barrels in the lit glass case.

"It makes me feel something," Claude said hesitantly.

"Everything's fried here. It's amazing."

"Do they have a salad?"

"A fried salad! But you should try the catfish. It's so good," I said enthusiastically.

"When's my workout?"

"I'm sure it's not for a few days," I said, reaching for my phone. Reading the message from Papa, I said, "It's tomorrow morning at 9 AM."

"Wow, that's quick," Claude responded nervously.

"It is," I admitted, hearing the deafening footsteps as the end of our friendship approached. "Maybe this isn't the best place. We'll come here for our celebratory dinner after you make the team," I said, further building his expectations.

Leaving there, we found the healthiest restaurant we could. Claude ordered two skinless chicken breasts over lettuce while I ate something with flavor. An hour after that, we headed to the park to loosen him up.

There was no point in doing drills past throwing the ball around. He wasn't going to gain anything from one practice 18 hours before the workout. The best we could hope for was for him to get a good night's sleep. So, that's what we did.

Getting back to my place before dark, I set Claude up with sheets and one of my pillows, and then headed to bed. I desperately needed sleep, and again it didn't come. By the time the sun shone in through my window, I felt like I was going insane.

All night, I kept thinking about what would happen if things didn't go well today. I had just gotten Claude back. I wasn't ready to lose him again. Everything had to go perfectly. I couldn't be sure what I would do if they didn't.

Dragging myself out of bed, I met Claude in the living room. He was sitting on the couch dressed with his folded sheets and pillow next to him.

"Sleep well?" I asked, sounding like I had swallowed a frog.

"I got a few hours," he replied, not looking rested.

"Was the couch not comfortable?" I asked in a panic.

"No, it was fine," he reassured me. Then he closed his eyes, took a deep breath, and said, "Thoughts."

I wasn't sure why, but him saying that made me feel a little better.

"I get it. How do you feel? You feel ready?"

His head barely moved as he nodded. He wasn't going to let me in. Even now, as I felt like I would explode, he was a locked box of emotions. Nothing got out.

Or, maybe I was putting more weight on this than it deserved. Maybe he truly didn't give a shit whether things went well at the workout. Maybe he had seen enough of me and my child-like life to know that he wanted no part of it or football.

"Can you eat breakfast?" I asked, knowing I wouldn't keep anything down if I tried.

"Something light. And maybe some coffee. I usually run in the mornings. How about I do a mile or two and stop somewhere on the way? It will help clear my head."

"I can go with you," I offered, knowing I would collapse after a block but wanting to be with him.

"No, I need to get my mind right for the workout. How long will it take to drive where we're going?"

"Twenty minutes?"

"Then I'll be back in an hour."

"Right," I said, watching him go.

More time to think was the last thing I needed. So instead, I made a list of all of the things Papa and the general manager would be looking for from Claude. It was an exhaustive list. Or, more precisely, I was exhausted, and the words I wrote created a list.

Who was I kidding? This wasn't going to distract me from anything. So instead, I sat on the couch, turned on the PlayStation, and fell asleep. I knew why I had. The couch smelled like Claude. It was like his arms were wrapped around me.

"Merri," Claude said, waking me up. "Shouldn't we head out?"

I looked at the clock above the TV. "We have forty minutes," I said groggily.

"Being on time is late," he reminded me.

Staring up at him, I liked the way he looked. I mean, I always liked the way he looked. What I meant this time was that he looked ready.

"Yeah, we should go."

Getting dressed and driving over, I was still too tired to be stressed. But entering the stadium, it hit me. This was going to be it. In a few hours, the rest of my life would be set. Either I was going to be unemployed and Claude would again be gone from my life. Or, I would have everything I ever wanted. My chest tightened at the prospect.

"Claude!" Papa said, shaking his hand with a smile. "Do you feel ready for this?"

Claude gave Papa a million-dollar smile. "As I'll ever be."

"Good. I expect great things from you," Papa said, having never said that to me.

"I'll do my best."

"That should be enough."

Yep, Papa had his favorite son back. 'Good for him,' I thought sarcastically.

"I'll take Claude to the field. Who's gonna run the workout?"

"Vincent," Papa said, giving me a nod. "Good luck."

"Thanks," I said at the same time as Claude. They both looked at me. "Oh, you meant him. Right. I didn't get much sleep. Jetlag."

Claude tilted his head, reminding me that Tennessee and Florida were only an hour apart.

"Follow me," I said, escorting him to the edge of the practice field. "Vincent's our quarterback coach. Papa runs a lot of the same plays he ran with you. Do you remember them?"

"For the most part."

"That'll help."

"Are you okay?" he asked, looking at me concerned.

How was I supposed to respond? Should I tell him that, despite what I had promised myself I would do, I was practically going blind with the stress of whether or not he would leave me again?

"I'm fine. You just stay focused. You know everything Vincent is going to run you through. You've done them all a hundred times in practice. And don't worry, you're going to be great," I said sincerely, knowing it was true no matter the outcome.

"Thanks," he said with one of his brilliant smiles. It was enough to make me think that everything would be alright.

Retreating to the sidelines, my stomach churned from nerves. Watching Claude and Vincent talk, I could barely breathe. As Claude ran through the routine, I looked up into the stands. The only ones in it were Papa, the general manager, and the team's owner.

"Fuck!"

I guess it was naive of me to think that he wouldn't be. Still, a boy could dream. It wasn't like he would hold something against Claude because we had a history. The old man wouldn't know anything about it. As long as Claude did what he was capable of and Papa endorsed him, Claude should be fine.

After an excruciating hour and a half, Vincent took his clipboard full of notes to the decision makers. Meeting Claude on the field, my heart thumped like a jackrabbit's.

"What'd he say?" I asked him.

This was it. Either my career was over, and I was going to lose Claude forever, or I wasn't. I struggled to breathe.

"He said, good job and wait here," Claude said, still dripping with sweat.

"That's better than 'get the hell out,'" I joked, feeling a glimmer of hope.

"I guess."

"How do you think you did?"

"I missed my split a couple of times. I also think my passing was a little off. I should have practiced more. I don't know what I was thinking coming here. I'm not in NFL shape.

"Yeah, I'm good enough to throw the ball around with friends. But I don't think I was ready for this," he said, showing me more vulnerability than I had seen out of him in the three years we had been friends.

Without thinking, I grabbed his hand.

"Hey, look at me. You fuckin' rocked. Do you hear me? Even two-thirds of you is better than 100% of others. You are the best quarterback I've ever seen, and if they can't see that, fuck 'em," I said, meaning it.

Claude looked up. His eyes were soft and gentle. I was seeing a side of him that I had never seen before. It made me weak in the knees.

"You are the best," I told him. "Truly. I mean it. I've never met a better man than you."

"Thanks," he said sincerely.

Then I did something I shouldn't have. On the field in front of whoever was watching, I gave him a hug. It wasn't a bro-styled half-hug with our fists between our chests to make sure everyone knew we weren't gay. It was a long, lingering hug that spoke of things unsaid.

It was intimate and warm. It made me think that maybe this wasn't the end. Maybe it was just the beginning.

"Shit!" I heard someone behind me say.

I quickly let Claude go and turned around. It was the team's owner, and he looked disgusted. Turning to the general manager, he said, "He's another fuckin'

Mary, isn't he? Get him out of here," he ordered before walking away.

Panic hit me. "What?"

"Thanks for coming in," the general manager said, approaching Claude.

"What just happened?" I asked, knowing something had changed. Everyone wouldn't have come down to meet Claude if they didn't think he had done well. Not letting this go, I ran past Papa and got in front of the owner.

"What's going on? You know he was good."

The owner looked at me with bitter, bloodshot, old man's eyes and said, "This team doesn't need another Mary," and then pushed past me.

"What does that mean?" I asked before it hit me.

It was the hug. It was my non-bro hug.

"You aren't considering him because you think he's gay. You think because I'm gay, and I hugged him, he's gay too... you bigot."

The owner froze and stared at me, shocked. There was an unwritten rule with bigots. It's that they can insinuate things all day long. But as long as they don't say it directly, they can't be held accountable for it. Well, fuck that! I continued.

"Because I'm gay and you saw us hugging," I said, emphasizing how ridiculous it was, "you think he's gay too. And that's why you don't want him on the team, you fucking bigot!"

Dumbstruck, the owner looked back at Papa, Vincent, and the manager and then back at me. For a second I thought he was going to back down. I had trapped him. What I had said was true, and he knew it.

But when wounded animals are cornered, they don't give up. They attack.

Stiffening his spine, he gathered himself. As if I had never said it, he replied, "I'm dismissing him because your friend there can't pass, is as slow as molasses, and can't do a split to save his life."

"He can. He just needs more time to get ready. Before I went up there, he hadn't touched a football in two years."

"What?" The old man said, suddenly on the defensive.

"That's right. That's how good he is with time off. Imagine how good he'll be once someone works with him."

I thought I had him. His fangs had retracted. His venom was gone. Turning to me calmly, he said,

"Then I guess you should have thought about that before scheduling the workout, shouldn't you?" He told me, making everything that was happening my fault.

Having rocked me back onto my heels, the old man walked off. I didn't know what else to say. Turning to Papa, I headed towards him.

"You had asked me to bring him as soon as I could."

In front of Claude, he said, "But you didn't tell me that he hadn't touched a ball in two years. What were you thinking bringing him here? You knew that bastard was looking for any excuse to make our lives harder. You didn't have to help him."

"But you told me to bring him as soon as I could," I repeated, feeling my resistance slip away.

"I did. But sometimes you gotta think, Son," he said as if I were the biggest idiot in the world.

Papa turned to Claude and offered him his hand.

"Thanks for coming down, Claude. It was truly good to see you. I'm sorry things didn't work out," he said with genuine disappointment in his smile.

"You too, Coach," Claude replied as if to him, none of this was a big deal.

Once everyone had offered Claude their tight-lipped smiles and had left, I turned to my once best friend. With tears pooling in my eyes, I said, "I'm sorry."

"Can we go?" was his only reply.

Neither of us said a word as we walked back to my car. The silence continued until I opened my mouth to speak, and he cut me off.

"Can you reschedule my return flight? If I can, I would like to leave tonight."

A chill washed through me. Everything I feared was coming true.

"But, why? You don't have anything you need to rush back to, do you? You can stay with me. We could catch up," I said, feeling my world fall apart.

"Merri, I need to go. Can you change my return flight, or do I have to buy a new one?"

"I can change it," I told him, trying to hide the tears that rolled down my cheeks.

Back at my place, neither of us spoke. Changing his return flight and then watching him gather his stuff, I said, "At least let me take you to dinner. Can we do that?"

"I'm gonna head out," he replied as if none of this meant anything to him.

"I'll take you to the airport."

"I ordered an Uber."

"So, is this it?" I asked, no longer able to hide the tears.

Claude didn't answer. He just said, "Bye, Merri," and walked out of my life.

It was only then that I let loose everything I was holding back. Falling to the ground, I cried. I thought it had hurt the first time he had left me. But that was nothing compared to what I felt now.

Chapter 10

Claude

Why had I let myself want it? I was a fool to think that anything Merri was telling me was true. I knew I wasn't as good as I used to be. I could feel it. Yet, I chose to believe him. I had trusted him when I knew that the only person I could trust was myself.

Now I felt like my insides were being torn out. I didn't want this. I hadn't wanted this. But getting a taste of it, I craved it like nothing I had felt before.

What was it that I wanted so badly? Was it to get back onto a football team? Was it to once again feel like I mattered? I didn't know. All I did know was that I hurt and I didn't know how to stop the pain.

On the way to the airport, I held myself together. The same was true as I waited for my flight and boarded the plane. With hours to remember how I had escaped these feelings before, I did my best to push down my heartache and disappointment.

By the time I had landed in Tennessee, I had realized that it wasn't working. None of my techniques for going numb were working. I could still feel all of it, the unworthiness, the loneliness, they were all floating just below the surface.

At any moment, I felt like I was going to explode. The only thing left for me to do was to pretend none of it had happened. I would tell no one about it. I would try not to think about it again.

'How's it going in Florida?' a text from Titus read as I rode the bus from Knoxville.

"Shit!"

I wasn't going to be able to pretend like none of it had happened. Everyone knew it had. Merri had told everyone about it, ensuring that I would never be able to escape the questions. My only respite would come by hiding in my room, and the thought of that made me want to peel the skin off my bones.

I was trapped. Merri had trapped me. I could no longer run from my feelings. Cowering in the corner like a scared child, I looked up at them.

The monster was dark and terrifying. Without mercy, it consumed me. And with nowhere else to run, I fell forward in my bus seat and bawled.

It wasn't just for the workout that I had cried. It was for everything. It was for hearing my best friend call me what he had. It was for the pain I felt bottling up my loneliness. It was for the eight-year-old who couldn't have fun with his friends because he had had the reputation of his entire race put on his shoulders.

With the tears flowing, it didn't feel like they would stop. But it was a long bus ride between Knoxville and home. And getting off the bus at the closest stop 20 miles out of town, I retreated to the nearest bench, put my elbows on my knees, and my face in my hands.

I had made a mess of so many things. What was my life? Who did I have? How had I ended up alone?

Looking at my phone when it buzzed, Titus's text read, 'BTW, Lou says that when you start playing for the Cougars, he's gonna stage a corporate takeover of the tour company.'

Seconds later he wrote, 'Now he's telling me I wasn't supposed to tell you that.'

Seconds after that, 'Now he's saying that he will never have sex with me again if I don't tell you that he didn't say that. So, he definitely didn't say that.'

Seconds after that, 'Hey Claude, this is Lou. Titus is just kidding around. You know how he likes to kid. How's the workout going? Are you their starting quarterback yet? No hidden agenda behind the question. Asking for a friend.'

Reading Titus's last message, I couldn't help myself. I laughed. It was enough to remind me that my world wasn't coming to an end.

Sitting up, I took a deep breath. Staring at my phone again, I called Titus.

"Claude, how's it going?"

"To be honest, not great."

"What's the matter?" My brother asked, concerned.

"Could you pick me up at the airport bus stop?"

"You're back?"

"Yeah."

"I'll be there as soon as I can," he told me, with enough sadness in his voice to tell me I wouldn't have to explain anything else.

I was relieved. Maybe I would be able to pretend like none of this had happened. Perhaps I would be able to return my life to what it had been.

Hadn't I finally been included in Cage's social circle? Couldn't I turn that invitation into a life that was worth living? If I could get through today without talking about things, I could take it one day at a time. Eventually, this would all be a distant memory.

When Titus's truck pulled up, I was relieved to see that it was only him in it. I liked Lou but he was often a bit much. He wouldn't be able to stop himself from asking about every detail of what had happened. I couldn't handle that now.

I just wanted a ride home without having to talk about anything. I wanted to move on from everything that had happened. I wanted that… making what happened next so surprising.

"How do you do it?" I asked my brother, breaking the silence.

"How do I do what?" Titus asked soberly.

"How do you make life seem so easy?"

He looked at me, surprised.

"You think my life is easy?"

"No. That's just it. You're a star player on your football team, you part-own a business, you're mayor of this town, you have a boyfriend, and yet you have this tremendous social group. It can't be easy to do all of that. Yet, you make it look like it is."

"I'm glad you think so. And you're right, it's a lot. But, everything's a lot easier when you're willing to ask for help. I know I can't handle all of this on my own. But I have people like you and Lou to help me out. I know you would be there if I need you to. Just like I would be there for you."

Hearing his words, I lowered my eyes.

"I didn't make the team. They said I wasn't good enough."

"That sucks," Titus said empathetically.

"Yeah."

After a moment, Titus said, "Can I ask you a question?"

"What's that?"

"Why didn't you tell anyone you played football at university?" Titus asked delicately.

I opened my mouth to speak. I was going to say, I don't know. But I stopped myself, knowing it wasn't the truth.

"I have a problem opening up," I told him honestly.

"Why is that?"

"God knows. I could say it was because of something my mother said to me when I was eight. Or because I didn't feel like I had anyone I could trust growing up. Or maybe it's because I just don't know who I am and I don't want people to see that."

"That's rough," Titus said, nodding empathetically.

"I don't want to be like this anymore."

"Be like what?"

"Distant. Alone. I don't want to carry everything on my shoulders anymore. I want to be able to open up."

"Then, why don't you?"

"I don't know how. I've tried. I try to share things. I even come up with rules where I'm required to break my habits. But every time I'm in the situation and I know I have the opportunity, I choose not to. I can't do it."

"Sure you can," Titus said encouragingly.

"I can't. Believe me, I've tried. I tried with Merri."

"And what happened?"

"He asked if we could pretend it didn't happen."

Titus thought for a moment.

"You like Merri, don't you?"

"Yeah," I admitted, defeated.

"I mean, in the way I like Lou."

I nodded. "Yeah."

"He seemed like a nice guy."

"He has his moments."

"Do you think he feels the same way about you?"

"I know he used to."

"Have you told him how you feel?"

"You mean with words?"

Titus laughed.

"Yeah, with words."

"I'm not great at that."

"You should practice."

"What do you mean?"

Titus shrugged, regaining his usually upbeat tone.

"It's like football, isn't it?"

"How so?"

"You didn't start off as a crazy good quarterback, did you?"

"No."

"And, how did you get good?"

"Hard work. Study. Practice."

"Exactly. How much have you practiced telling people how you feel about them?"

As I opened my mouth, I felt a pain in my chest. Even the thought of it was overwhelming.

"What? Too much?" Titus asked, stealing a glance at me from the road.

I huffed satirically.

"Okay, it's too much right now. Just like how a perfect Hail Mary pass might be too much to expect the first time you picked up a football. But, you could throw a short pass, right? And if the receiver stepped further back each time and you kept practicing, eventually you'd have it."

"So, you're saying that if I had practiced, I would have been able to tell Merri how I felt?"

"I'm saying that if you practice, you still could," he said with a smile.

"How does one practice opening up?"

Titus tightened his lips, searching for a reply.

"You start with little things like compliments. How often do you give people compliments?"

"I give them when I think people deserve them."

"Which I'm assuming is not very often?"

I chuckled.

"I'm only assuming that because I've never heard one from you. So, I'm hoping that's the case."

"What are you talking about? I compliment you all the time."

"Name once."

I opened my mouth and then chuckled.

"Don't worry. I don't take it personally. It's just who you are."

"But, you shouldn't have to make excuses for my being a bad brother."

"I didn't say that. You're the best brother I could've hoped for. Don't tell Cali, but you're my favorite," he said, blushing.

"Thanks." I paused. "You too."

Titus looked at me and leadingly asked, "Me too, what?"

"You want me to say it?" I asked him, confused.

"Yes, Claude! That's the point of what I was saying. You need to practice it. And since I'm picking you up, making me obviously a great brother, this should be a short pass."

"You're a good brother, too," I conceded.

Titus smiled. "Thanks, Claude. I really appreciate you saying it."

"Well, it's true," I confirmed. "You've been a good brother to me."

"Thanks. So, how painful was that to say?"

"It wasn't that bad," I admitted.

"Now, do that a thousand more times and in a few years, you might be able to tell Merri he has great hair," Titus teased.

"Fuck you," I joked.

"What? Too much. How about satisfactory hair? Do you think in a couple of years, you might be able to work up to that?"

"Fuck you, Titus," I said with a smile.

He laughed.

As much sense as Titus had made, that didn't change the bind I was in. Thanks to Merri, everyone knew where I had gone and I was going to have to tell everyone I had failed.

"How was your trip?" My mother asked me when I arrived home. "Did you help out your friend?"

"I did," I told her.

"That's good. Did you get laid?"

"Momma!"

"I just figured that if you were sneaking off to 'help' a 'friend' that you've never mentioned before, my baby boy was finally gonna see some action."

"Oh my God, Momma! And I wasn't sneaking off. I told you where I was going."

"Sure you did," Momma said with a smile.

Staring at her, knowing she wasn't completely wrong, I wondered if she was the reason I couldn't share anything with anyone. I never questioned whether or not she loved me. But, like Titus's boyfriend, Lou, Momma was a lot.

"I'm going to my room," I informed her before collecting my travel bag and heading upstairs.

Lying in bed, staring at the small shadows cast by the setting sun on the textured ceiling, I wondered what I was supposed to do next. In one day, I had lost both the career and the man that I had wanted so badly that I couldn't admit it.

And, wasn't it because I couldn't admit to it that I had lost them? If I had practiced instead of denying my feelings, wouldn't I now have everything I had ever wanted?

If I had a second chance to do it all again, I would do everything differently. Too bad I didn't have that chance… Or did I?

Chapter 11

Merri

Sleep. I needed sleep. And once I dragged myself off the ground and into bed, I got it. When I awoke, I saw things in a different light. Literally. I had been so exhausted, that when I woke up, it was past midnight. Having gone 48 hours on 45 minutes of sleep, I had a lot of catching up to do.

"Oh shit! Claude," I said, remembering everything that had happened.

He had left furious at me. And like the last time, he had the right to be. Was I even capable of not hurting him? What was it about me that made me keep doing this?

Was it how badly I wanted him? Did my obsession with him blind me to reason?

Yes, he wasn't ready for the workout. I could see that. He wasn't far off, but he wasn't there yet. If I had been more patient and perhaps considered how my actions would have affected him, I could have made better choices.

But, I had ruined it. I had ruined us. And there was no going back.

Wasn't I also fired? Searching for my phone, I expected a message saying exactly that. I didn't have one. I wasn't sure why. Hadn't I called my boss a bigot in front of everyone? Wasn't that grounds for termination even if it was true?

Whatever the reason I hadn't yet been fired, I was sure it was a matter of time until I was. Not only did the team's owner not want me there, but I had failed the coach. Claude was truly the best shot Poppa had at keeping his job. Rushing Claude into the workout had screwed over everyone. Now everyone was unhappy, and I was to blame.

"Shit!" I muttered in the darkness.

I didn't know what to do. How did I get myself out of this? How did I make things right?

I didn't leave bed that night. Instead, I thought. As the sun rose, I became acutely aware that I hadn't eaten in days. I wouldn't say that I had an appetite, but I was interested in not dying… barely.

Seriously, how had I gotten myself into this mess? I was at a complete loss. Was I just broken? Was I incapable of doing anything right?

With nothing in my fridge besides condiments, I did my best to pull myself together and get something to eat. There weren't a lot of places that were open at this hour. But I did know of one place that would be soon. It was a short walk away. Maybe the fresh air would do me good.

Leaving my building, headed for the historic part of Pensacola, my mind wandered. What must it have been like to live here a hundred and fifty years ago? Could there have been a man who walked the same path, thinking the same things as I was?

Surrounded by the stone buildings and quaint stores, I found the breakfast café I had once gone to. Waiting for it to open, I thought about the last time I was here. It was months ago, after a night at my ex's place. He had asked me if I wanted to see his favorite breakfast spot. This had been it. So whenever I saw it, I thought about,

"Merri?" A familiar voice said, turning me around.

"Jason?" I said, staring into my ex's eyes.

Immediately pissed, Jason crossed his arms defiantly.

"I was the one who introduced you to this spot. This is my spot. I'm not leaving."

"I'll go," I conceded, knowing he was right.

As I walked away, I thought about what it meant that I would run into him now. It wasn't like he came here every day. He traveled almost as much as I did.

"Wait, can I talk to you for a second?" I asked, turning around.

He exhaled exhaustively. "What?" he snapped.

I lowered my head. "I didn't handle things well with you."

"No shit," he confirmed.

"Right. And, I guess I would like to apologize for it."

Jason looked at me, confused. "What's going on here?"

"I'm apologizing for being a piece of shit to you; for being a piece of shit in general," I said, with my eyes welling up.

Jason looked at me heartlessly. That lasted until he threw his head back and groaned, annoyed.

"Although I would like you to feel like a piece of shit, you're not a piece of shit, Merri."

"You're saying that because you don't know me. I ruin people's lives. I'm a selfish asshole," I admitted, failing to hold back my tears.

"No, you're not."

"But I am," I insisted.

"Merri, it's hard enough not hating you right now. Don't make me have to say nice things about you. You hurt me. It's taking a lot out of me to not let you beat yourself up."

"I'm sorry. See, I'm not good."

"Would you like to know what your problem is, Merri?"

"What's that?"

"You're empty," he said accusingly.

"What?"

"You heard me. You have this hole inside of you that you keep trying to fill with things. You think that if you're the perfect gay, the football gods will like you, and it will fill your hole. Well, I tried to fill your hole, Merri. I tried really hard. But your hole is bigger than the both of us."

Jason stopped as an old woman walked by, staring at him.

"It was a metaphor," he yelled at her. He turned to me. "You know what I meant."

"I'm not sure I do," I said honestly.

He looked at me, clenching his jaw. Calming himself, he explained.

"You don't feel like a whole person. Probably because your father never accepted you for who you are. So now you're going to spend the rest of your life chasing after what you couldn't get as a kid. And when one thing can't give it to you, you'll put all of your attention on something else, like, oh, I don't know, the acceptance of a bunch of football players in a league that doesn't give two shits about you."

"Or, a straight best friend I can't get over," I realized.

Jason stared at me with his mouth hanging open. "Of course he is. I knew there was someone else. And I should have known he was straight. The harder you have to struggle to get it, the better, right? You couldn't just love the guy in front of you offering it. You have to fight for it to make it feel real." Jason winced. "I hate it when my therapist is right."

I stared at my ex, amazed. "If that's true, then what do I do about it? Because I'm seriously out of ideas."

"Here's a thought. And this might sound crazy. But instead of just focusing on what you need, why don't you try doing something for someone else for a change? And not because it's going to get you something. But because it will help them. Have you tried that?" He asked snarkily.

Jason looked around and then back at me.

"You know what, I don't even want to eat here anymore. You can have it. I have too much going on to deal with this," he said before turning around and storming off.

Watching Jason walk away, I was stunned. I would have liked to believe that the grim picture he painted of me wasn't true, but it felt real. Wasn't what he said the reason I was obsessed with Claude?

From the moment I saw him, it was his difference that drew me to him. I was just some puny white kid from a small town in Oregon. He was this incredibly cool

Black guy who was athletic, good-looking, and had his shit together. On top of that, he was straight.

If I could get someone like that to like me, wouldn't that prove that what my father said about me wasn't true? Wouldn't having Claude as a best friend prove my worth? So when my feelings for him threatened to ruin everything, I flipped out. I lost my mind because who was I without him?

Oh God, Jason was right. I'm just this black hole looking for things to fill it. Did I even love Claude, or did I just love the idea of him? I wasn't sure anymore. The only thing I was sure of was that I was starved. So as soon as Jason's breakfast spot opened, I ordered one of everything and tried to fill another hole.

Having been given a lot to think about, I returned home after my meal and thought about it all. That lasted until I fell asleep, which was around the same time I had fallen asleep the day before. Apparently, not sleeping for 48 hours can throw off your sleeping schedule.

But, in a way, it was good. Waking up after dark and going to sleep before noon gave me a lot of alone time. It helped me figure a few things out. For one, I hadn't just used Claude to feel better about myself. He and I genuinely had a good time together. We laughed when we were together, and we had shared interests.

That didn't mean that what Jason had said wasn't true. It was. Being with Claude validated me in a way that I can't fully explain.

But, was that wrong? Wasn't it good to feel lucky to be with the person you're with? Isn't that a sign that your relationship will last?

Perhaps where I went wrong was when I made Claude everything and not just a part of who I was. If Claude was everything, then losing him meant that I would lose everything. There had to be a part of me that remained without him. And, as Jason said, I had to start treating him like a friend and not just the person who validated me.

Oh shit, I have screwed so many things up. But I was done wallowing about it. I didn't want to be that guy any more. I wanted to be better, for Claude. Even if he didn't want to be friends anymore, I wanted to help him be happy. What would make Claude happy?

As I fought to realign my sleeping schedule, I thought about this. On the day that I woke up at 9 AM, it was with an answer. Although he was reluctant to say it, he had admitted that he wanted to play football again. I had torpedoed his chance at playing for the Cougars, but I still believed he was a generational talent.

If he was properly trained and back to where he was when he won us our third Division II title, he would make an NFL team. The question was, how could NFL scouts see him play to recommend him to their teams? If he was still a student, I could invite scouts to games. But, having graduated early, he forfeited his college eligibility.

That was when it hit me. I knew exactly how I could get NFL scouts to see him. And, I knew who could make it happen.

"Oh God, what is it?" Jason said when he answered my call.

"I've been thinking about what you said to me. And I would like to apologize again for being such a bad boyfriend to you. Everything you said about me was right. I do have a big hole, and you couldn't fill it. No one person could."

"I think it sounds worse when you say it," Jason said, unmoved by my apology.

"In any case, I've decided I'm going to start focusing on the needs of others and not just mine."

"This is progress," he said, perking up.

"And, I would like to start by helping you."

"Really? This ought to be good. Go on."

"What if I told you that I have an NFL prospect that none of the other scouting agencies know about, but would be the number one draft pick if they did?"

Jason paused.

"This is about the straight boy, isn't it?"

I winced.

"Yes. But, he is also the best quarterback you will ever see."

"This hardly sounds like something for me. It sounds a lot like something you want me to do for you," Jason warned.

"It's not. Well, it kind of is. But not because I'm going to get something out of it. This guy really is the best quarterback I have ever seen in my life. He's the reason my father got the job with the Cougars."

"Wait, is this the guy you would talk about from your university team? The one who would do the trick plays?"

"The trick plays that led to three national titles."

"Merri, they were Division II titles. Me and the bench at Harvard could win one," he said dismissively.

"Okay, but he won all the games in front of him. That's all you can do, right? Beat the teams you're playing? And he did. Think about what he could have done if he played in Division One."

"And why wasn't he in Division One?"

"Because his freshman year was the first time he ever played quarterback."

"What?"

"Yeah. He tried out for the team as a walk-on and didn't think to try out for quarterback. He only did because, well, I forced him to."

"What are his stats?"

"Through the roof."

"No, Merri. I need his actual stats."

"If I get them to you, and you like them, would you consider including him in your pre-season player showcase?"

"The showcase is only for college students who weren't drafted," Jason said.

"But you help organize it. You could make an exception."

"Merri, why are you doing this?"

"Why am I giving you the opportunity of a lifetime?" I said, entering pure salesman mode.

"Come on, Merri, I'm serious."

I paused.

"It's because I want to do something that helps him and not just me. Claude was my best friend. He was good to me, and I wasn't always good to him. But he is talented and deserves to have a shot at his dream. If I can do that for him, maybe it will make up for when I wasn't so good."

"So, this would still be for you?"

"As much as it is for you. Let's be real, if you find the player no one else could, and he blows up, yours will become the scouting agency the teams rely on. This could benefit all of us. But, I'm doing this for him."

Jason was silent on the other end of the phone. I was thinking that I had lost him until he said,

"Send me his stats. If they're anything like you're claiming…"

"They are."

"Then I'll see what I can do."

"Thank you, Jason. And I'm truly sorry things didn't work out between us."

"Yeah. Whatever," he replied before hanging up.

Compiling everything I had on Claude, I emailed them to Jason. It took a few days, but eventually he replied, 'Not bad. I'll see what I can do.'

That was step one. Step two was going to be far harder. I was going to have to convince Claude to stop hating me long enough to consider another offer.

Chapter 12

Claude

Titus had been right. Practice did make things easier. I wasn't yet up to the compliment phase, but I was at the accepting invitations phase. So when Cage invited me to his and Quin's next game night, I said yes. More than that, I went.

Almost everyone was there. It was a good time. My team even won a game.

Apparently, that was a near miracle because no one ever beat whatever team Quin was on. I don't know what the big deal was, but according to Nero, that earned me a lifetime membership to the club. I felt bad for Quin, though. Everyone was making such a big deal that my team won that it couldn't have felt good for him.

Anyway, driving home still feeling the alcohol, I felt pleased with myself. I was making progress. I was opening up, even if just a little. And already my life was better for it. Now, the only thing I had to worry about was,

"Merri!" I yelped, opening my front door to find him at the kitchen table talking to Momma. "What are you doing here?"

He winced. "Screwing things up?"

"Your 'friend' here was just telling me how you 'helped' him. You worked out for an NFL team?" Momma asked, shocked.

"Sorry," Merri offered mournfully. "I should have realized she wouldn't know. I just thought…"

"No, Merri, this is not your fault. It's mine. Yes, Momma, he's the friend I went to visit. He was in town a few weeks ago to ask me to workout for the NFL team he's the assistant coach on. I don't know why I didn't tell you."

Momma stared at me blankly. "So, let me get this straight, you had a friend in college? This whole time I thought I had raised a pariah. How many more friends have you had? Is Claude even your real name?"

I chuckled.

"That's the name my momma gave me."

"Is it? Because I don't even know anymore."

"Momma, can I talk to Merri alone?"

"So, you admit that your friend has a name. And you didn't think to mention it all this time."

"Please, Momma."

She got up. Approaching me, she said, "Remember what I said about the bedroom window," and then headed upstairs.

Alone with Merri, I turned to him.

"What are you doing here?" I asked, trying not to sound harsh.

"I needed to talk to you."

"You know, they've invented this thing called a phone."

"I thought you deserved to hear this in person."

I considered what he said, nodded, and then replied, "You look nice, by the way."

It took a second for him to respond. When he did, it was as a deer would staring into the headlights of a truck.

"What?" He eventually asked.

"I said, you look nice," I repeated with a nervous smile.

Merri shook his head, trying to rattle things back into place.

"I'm sorry. You just threw me for a second. I've never heard those words come out of your mouth before. It took me a moment to figure out what they meant."

"What are you talking about? I've said you look nice before."

Merri feigned thinking about it before saying, "No. I was in love with you for three years. I think I would remember that."

"So, I've never complimented you before?" I asked, surprised.

Merri pretended as if he had remembered something and then said, "Nope. Not once. Not even that time when I wore a tuxedo and looked an awful lot like James Bond."

"Oh, I remember that," I said with a smile.

He stared at me, waiting for something. "And?"

"And what?"

Merri sighed. "Nothing. Look, I'm here because I want to make you another offer."

"Did the Cougars' owner reconsider?" I asked, feeling a tingling in my chest.

"Oh. No. He's still a bigot and a dick."

"Oh."

"The offer I want to make involves a pre-season showcase."

"A pre-season showcase?"

"Yeah. There's a showcase for undrafted players held in the middle of pre-season. I've been pulling a few strings, and I think I can get you included."

"Why would you do that?" I asked, unsure how to feel.

"Because, despite how much you pretend not to want to play for the NFL, I think you do. I think you want it a lot. And I might have screwed things up for you with the Cougars, but you could still make it on a team. You could become the best quarterback in the history of the league; I just wouldn't be your assistant coach," he said with a sad smile.

I didn't know how to feel about that. One of the only reasons I played football was for Merri. I had wanted to show off for him. What would football be without him?

"But, you heard your team's owner. I'm slow to my spots and I can't make a split to save my life."

"Yeah, but he also believes that gays shouldn't be involved with football. So, I would hardly call him a reliable source of information."

"But I feel it. I feel slow," I admitted.

"And that brings us to the other part of my offer."

"Which is?"

"I would like you to stay at my place for the summer while I train you. I guess you don't have to stay at my place. You can stay anywhere. But, my place is free. And since I still have access to the Cougars' facilities, I could use it to prepare you."

"For the summer?"

"Until the showcase."

"I have a business to run."

"That's right. You do," he said, remembering. "Could your brother cover for you? I mean, if he knew how much it meant to you?"

"Assuming I want it?"

"Of course. I would completely understand if you didn't. You have a life here. You have friends and a spitfire of a mom. By the way, why did she ask me how good I was at climbing out of windows?"

I shrugged as if I didn't know.

"You're right. I do have a life here. At least, I could have one."

"I understand," he said, trying to hide his disappointment.

"But, Titus's boyfriend has already started making plans for a corporate takeover. So, he might be able to fill in for me while I'm gone."

"Really?" Merri asked, excited.

"Maybe. And I don't think I could afford my own place for the summer, considering I wouldn't be working, so I would need to stay at your place."

Merri bottled his reaction and said, "You would be welcome."

"You really think you can get me included in the showcase?"

"My ex owns a scouting agency. He and I are the founding members of the gay football mafia. We could get you in."

"Could you?" I said with a laugh.

"Not that I'm saying you're gay. I'm just saying, you have a pretty mouth there, Mr. Quarterback guy."

I froze.

"I'm kidding! That was a joke. It's what every creepy gay southerner says in movies. I don't think you have a pretty mouth. I mean, you do but… You know what, let's pretend I stopped talking after gay football mafia."

"Got it," I said, relaxing.

"So, what do you say?"

I thought about it.

"Do it!" My mother yelled from upstairs.

Merri and I looked at each other, shocked. He mouthed 'Wow'! And I apologetically agreed with him.

"I'll think about it," I told him before saying it again facing the stairs. "I'll think about it."

"Let him know that if he needs a place to stay…"

I cut Momma off before she could finish that. "I'm sure he has a place, Momma. Do you, Merri?" I asked, suddenly unsure.

"I do. I'm at Cali's place again."

"Okay. Because if you did need a place, you could stay here."

"We'd be happy to have you," Momma added.

"Thank you, Miss Harper," Merri replied before saying, "I'll go. But I want you to know that there's no pressure. If you truly want to play for an NFL team, this would be your best chance. And I know that if you wanted it, you could have it. I'd do everything in my power to make sure of that," he said with a smile.

"I'll talk to Titus and let you know."

"Tomorrow?"

"Tomorrow," I confirmed and then showed him out.

After watching him walk to his car and drive off, I returned to the kitchen to find Momma there. I was expecting her to make a big deal about everything, but she didn't.

"He seemed nice."

"He has his moments."

"You're smiling," she pointed out.

"Am I?"

"You are," she said with a smile. "Is this about the football or him?"

I shrugged and headed upstairs to my room.

The next morning I headed into the office knowing Titus would be there. We still had a few things to do to prepare our new place before the season started and not having class on Mondays, he had agreed to help.

"It was fun last night," I told him as we installed the glass case for our t-shirts.

"It was! And you know you've become a legend, right? We didn't even think it was possible to beat Quin at a game. You might have shaken his entire worldview."

"If you insist," I conceded. "So, something funny happened when I got home."

"What was that?"

"I had a guest."

Titus stopped working and stared at me. "Who?"

"Merri."

Titus tilted his head quizzically. "And?"

"And, he was there with an offer."

"From his team?"

"No. He has an ex who can get me into a special showcase."

"That's amazing."

"But, I would need to spend the summer with him training."

"Are you doing it?" Titus asked excitedly.

"I don't know. I have responsibilities here… with you."

"Are you talking about this place?"

"Yeah."

"Lou and I can handle it while you're gone," he said with a smile. "He's already been talking about ways he can be involved with the business. I think he's trying to get me to invite him to live with me."

"Oh, that's right. He's graduating this spring."

"Yeah," Titus said nervously.

"And?"

"I mean, I love him. Why wouldn't I invite him to move in? He loves the town. He loves Quin and Quin will be here. It just makes sense, right?"

"And how do you feel about it?"

Titus huffed.

"Nervous. I mean, that's a big step, isn't it?"

"Do you love him?"

"No doubt."

"Do you think you two will get along if you lived together?"

"I hope so. I know we have fun when we're together. It just feels like a lot to have him there every day."

"I get that," I admitted.

"What about you? You think you could live with Merri? For the summer, I mean? Do you think you two would get along?"

"At university, the two of us were inseparable."

"Just like me and Lou."

"So, I guess neither of us will have that hard of a time adjusting," I suggested.

"I guess we won't," Titus said with a smile.

"Are you going to invite Lou to move in?"

"I guess I'll have to. You know, with you being in Florida for the summer and all," he said with a smile.

I grabbed Titus in a hug. "Thanks. I appreciate you."

"I appreciate you too, bro," Titus told me, giving me the encouragement I needed to go.

It didn't take long before training with Merri felt like we were back at university. Our days were filled with wind sprints and passing drills while our nights were all about the PlayStation.

But as much effort as I was putting into training, it didn't feel like I was making any progress. Merri noticed the same thing, calling it a plateau. He kept reassuring me that I would push through it. But when more time passed and I hadn't, I started to doubt everything.

"It's nice to see that I can still beat you at something," Merri said, crushing me at Mario Kart.

"If I'd played all of the time instead of having a life, I would be that good too."

"I call bullshit! Because there was no way you ever had a life without me. You forget that I know you."

"Okay, you're right. After graduating I did spend most of my nights reading."

"Oh my God, I'm so sorry," he said painfully. "Leaving me forced you to read?"

"You say it like it was a life sentence," I pointed out, amused.

"But wasn't it? I mean, wasn't it just as bad?"

"You're an idiot."

"Look at you, full of compliments."

That made me freeze. As much as I had tried, I had also been failing at the other thing I was here to practice.

"Seriously though, you're a good guy for allowing me to stay here."

"Don't worry about it. It's my pleasure. It was either invite you or get a plant. I'm still not sure which has more personality," he teased.

"Thank you for that. But, no, seriously, I really appreciate what you're doing for me."

"Of course. No problem. I missed you. It feels good having you around again," he said with one of his cute Merri smiles.

Seeing it and then the look in his eyes, my heart suddenly pounded. The mood had changed. I could feel it.

"Speaking of what feels good," he began.

"Yeah," I replied, hoping I knew where this was leading.

"I think we might need a break."

"From what?" I asked nervously.

"Our routine. I couldn't help but notice that your numbers still aren't increasing."

I looked away, disappointed that this was what he was referring to.

"I noticed that too. Do you want me to head home?"

"Home? No! Why would you suggest that? I meant a break from working out."

"Oh! You mean a rest day."

"Yeah, a rest day. What did I say?"

"Well, what I heard was that you thought I sucked and you were giving up on me."

Merri laughed sarcastically.

"Claude, the day I give up on you, call somebody, because I've stopped breathing," he said vulnerably.

I blushed. "Then, what were you suggesting?"

"Something that will take your mind off of training."

I paused.

"You mean, like a date?" I asked with my heart in my throat.

He looked at me surprised.

"Oh, no. Not a date. Definitely not a date."

Hearing his words, my heart broke.

"Oh."

Seeing my reaction, Merri backpedaled.

"I mean, it's not like I wouldn't want to go on a date with you. You know how I've felt about you."

"Then, what is it?" I asked vulnerably.

"I mean, we should stay focused on getting you prepared, shouldn't we?"

"Right. Because that's the only reason you invited me here," I reminded myself.

"It's not the only reason," he said, giving me hope. "But getting you this opportunity is important for both of us. How about we just keep things the way they used to be? At least for now. I really want to do this for you, Merri. And I don't want to fuck things up."

"Of course. Let's not fuck things up."

"Right," he agreed, looking sadder than I felt.

We scheduled our day off – that definitely didn't include a date – for the following day. We had been training seven days a week since I had gotten there. A rest was overdue.

While Merri slept in the next morning, I took the opportunity to restart my morning runs. With all the sprinting I had been doing, the ten miles felt easy. That meant my mind was free to wander. What it settled on was how much I wished Merri and I were going on a real date.

Since arriving, I had decided that Merri no longer felt what he used to for me. He couldn't. After kissing him, he had refused to talk about it. He had asked if we could pretend it never happened. Imagine me wanting to talk about something and Merri not. How repulsed must he have been by my kiss?

Finishing my casual two-hour run that did little to clear my mind, I returned home to find Merri awake and worried about where I was.

"I thought you went home," he joked. At least, I thought it was a joke.

"No, I decided to do a run around the city. I haven't gotten the chance to see much of it."

"There's not much to see."

"Still, it was nice familiarizing myself with where I'm living."

"I guess," he conceded, looking away in thought.

Joining Merri for a leisurely breakfast at a place in the historical district, I decided that today would also be a cheat day. Not only did I have waffles, but I had fried chicken and a full glass of milk. I was stuffed by the time we rolled out of there at noon.

Walking back to his place, I could tell there was something on his mind. Though I knew this would have been the perfect place to ask what he was thinking and perhaps give him a compliment, I didn't. I wasn't sure why.

My openness practice was going as well as my football practices were. For some reason, I wasn't making progress on either. I was going to have to do better, though. I knew that. I was going to have to make more of an effort on the field and with Merri.

It wasn't like I didn't immediately think about how beautiful Merri was every morning when he left his bedroom. Like back at university, he acted like he was allergic to shirts. When we were home, he never wore one. And the guy had the body of a demi-god.

I don't mean Hercules, of course. Merri was much smaller than that. But his lean lines and rippling stomach gave me thoughts. After weeks of staring at them, I had to wonder about myself.

Why had I kissed him? Had I been swept up in the moment? Was I just giving Merri what I thought he wanted? I wasn't sure. But if I could talk to Merri about it, perhaps I could figure it out.

Returning to his place, Merri took off his shirt and we both buried ourselves in the couch. Streaming the latest action movie on Netflix, we watched it mindlessly, taking full advantage of our day off.

"Why didn't you ever furnish this place?" I asked, scanning the blank walls and empty floor space.

"What do you mean? I have a couch, a TV, and a bed. What else is there?"

"What about a painting? Or at least a poster of a painting?"

"That would involve getting up, going to the poster store, and deciding what to buy. Who has time for that," he said as he sat on the couch, watching a movie.

"Have you not furnished it because you don't know how long the job with the Cougars will last?"

"There is that," he confirmed.

"How long is your father's contract for?"

"It's supposed to be four years, but it has an out clause. If the team fires him, they would still have to pay him. Me? Not so much. I would be left with nothing."

"I still think you should decorate the place," I decided.

He looked at me curiously. "Why?"

"Living like this, it's like you're waiting to begin your life. You're living it. This is it. This is your life. Commit to it. Put something on the walls. You can always take it with you if you leave."

That was the end of our conversation. I couldn't tell what Merri was thinking. I wouldn't have had to guess if I had asked him about it. But again, I stayed silent.

What was wrong with me? I knew the baby steps I had to make, and I couldn't even do that. Maybe I was destined to be alone. If not be alone, then at least feel like I was.

Merri was a great guy. I felt more comfortable around him than anyone else I knew. Yet, I couldn't even ask him how he was feeling. Why? What was wrong with me?

With that movie over, we watched another. Switching to a reality dating show after that, Merri announced that he would take me somewhere where I could see the city.

"We're losing daylight," I told him, liking his idea.

"That's fine. The view's better at night."

"Oh," I said, wondering what he was planning. "Is this something I should get dressed for?"

"Will you need to wear pants? We'll be outside, so yes, you will."

I chuckled.

"No. I meant… You know what, never mind. I'll go take a shower," I told him.

"I would say, don't take long, but who am I kidding," he said, giving me a smile.

"Whatever," I told him, dismissing his latest jab at the length of my showers.

Vowing to get in and out as quickly as possible, I left the bathroom thirty minutes later to find that Merri wasn't there. "Well, it's not my fault if we're late," I told myself, returning to the bathroom to finish getting ready.

"My God!" Merri said, banging on the bathroom door. "Aren't I supposed to be the gay one?"

"I was ready thirty minutes ago," I said, leaving the bathroom to find him shirtless.

'Wow!' I thought without saying it.

"Where are we going again?" I asked him as he entered the bathroom past me.

"You'll see," he told me as he closed the door behind him.

Entering the living room, I looked over at the kitchen. There was something unusual about it. There was actual food in it. But not just any food. There were things that would make for a weird non-date.

"Where are we going?" I asked him again when he left the bathroom five minutes later.

"See. Now that's how you take a shower. Let me just get dressed and we'll go," he said, looking incredible wrapped in a towel.

Retrieving the basket from the kitchen counter, we headed to his car.

"So, you're really not going to tell me where we're going?" I asked both nervous and excited.

"I told you I was going to show you where we are."

"What does that mean?" I asked, my pulse building with intrigue.

He looked at me with a devilish smile. "You'll see."

Driving toward the coast and away from the setting sun, we found ourselves next to a bluff. Cutting across it and stopping at what looked like a national park, we parked the car and got out.

"Where are we?" I asked, confused.

"It's the Bay Bluffs. It's a preserve."

"It looks closed," I observed.

"Which is why we're taking the long way in," he said with a smile.

Retrieving the basket for him, he led us around the pine log fence into the thicket of trees. Walking for a few minutes, we eventually came upon a carpentered walkway. Continuing down the path past a wooded area that reminded me of home, we eventually spilled out onto a long, empty beach.

"This is Pensacola. It's the best the city has to offer," Merri said, gesturing toward the white sand and pool-blue water in front of us.

"It's beautiful," I admitted.

"Are you ready for something to eat? I picked up a few things at the store while you were in the shower," he said, retrieving the basket from me. "I also brought a blanket. Should I put it out?"

"Sure," I said, feeling my heartbeat quicken. "But it's going to be dark soon."

"I also brought candles," he said, pulling them out of the basket. "They have covers so they won't blow out. See," he said, showing me.

Watching him lay out the blanket and set up the candles, my heart pounded. This non-date was starting to feel an awful lot like a date date. And when he pulled out the bottle of wine and began pouring, I sat.

"I probably shouldn't," I said, feeling myself withdraw.

"One night of wine isn't going to hurt training. Besides, tonight is about relaxing. Relax," he said with a smile.

Taking the cup, I scanned the rest of what he brought. None of it was on my diet plan. Cheese, crackers, fatty meats, jams—it all looked incredible.

"You went all out," I told him, feeling my nerves kick in.

"I figured you've been working so hard that you deserve it. Are you gonna have some?"

I fought my desire to pull away. "I don't know."

"Please. For me."

Looking at him, I couldn't refuse. He could talk me into doing anything. I had no resistance to him.

"Of course," I said, stacking everything together. Taking a bite, I was surprised. "It's good!"

"It's called carbs," Merri joked.

"I like them," I retorted.

Merri laughed.

Eating and drinking as the sun set along the beach, the two of us got comfortable. I couldn't help but stare at him. He caught me doing it and didn't seem to mind.

With the sound of the waves softly kissing the shore and a gentle breeze in the air, he asked,

"What's your biggest unfulfilled dream?"

"My biggest unfulfilled dream?"

"Yeah, you know. What do you most regret not having done?"

I sipped the wine and thought about it.

"I think what I regret most is not developing superpowers."

Merri laughed.

"Come on. I'm serious."

"So am I."

"Okay then, tell me. Why do you regret not developing superpowers?"

"It's because if I had them, I would feel required to help people."

Merri looked at me, confused.

"You don't need superpowers to help people. You could just help them."

"That's easier said than done. I don't know if you know this about me, but I'm wound pretty tight."

"You don't say!" he said sarcastically.

"No, it's true. I know I hide it pretty well, but I am."

"I never would have guessed."

"Anyway, I don't love how tightly I'm wound. I look at other people, and I see how easily they can fit in or have a good time." I paused. "I wish I were more like that," I said, feeling the weight of my words.

When my gaze dipped, Merri put his hand on my leg. It surprised me. Looking up into his eyes, his empathy cracked the seal around my heart. Quickly gathering myself, I continued.

"All I was saying was that if I had developed superpowers, then I could take on a heroic persona who could help people. He could do the things I've always wanted to do but I have a hard time doing."

Merri rubbed my leg.

"I'll drink to that," he said with a smile.

He clinked my cup, and we both drank. My gulp was enough to finish what I had. Merri gave me a refill.

"So, what about you?" I asked him. "What's your biggest regret?"

Merri thought for a moment.

"My regret is that, in all the time we've known each other, I've not become more like you," he said vulnerably.

"You don't want to be like me," I quickly said.

"Yeah, who would want to be disciplined and someone who demands respect every time they enter a room?"

Softly I told him, "It's not everything it's cracked up to be."

Merri, who had moved his hand to get closer to me, said, "It is from where I'm sitting."

Staring into his eyes, I lost my breath. With my heart thumping and our lips moving closer, there was an explosion. I pulled away and looked up. There were fireworks, literal explosions in the sky.

"What's going on?" I asked Merri.

He smiled. "I wondered if you knew."

"Knew what?"

"It's the Fourth of July."

"Oh!" I replied, looking up.

Lying back and getting comfortable, Merri joined me. Crawling into my arms and resting his head on my chest, we watched together. Pulling him to me, I felt his warm body on mine. I didn't want this moment to end.

The explosions seemed to last forever, and when the fireworks stopped, Merri crawled up my chest and kissed me. Kissing him back, I parted his lips in search of his tongue. Finding it, our tongues danced.

I was kissing Merri, my best friend, my favorite person in the world, and it was incredible. My thoughts pulled and melted like caramel. Slipping my fingers into his hair, I massaged the back of his head.

I wanted him. I wanted every part of him. Gently pulling his lean, muscular arms, he climbed on top of me.

And when I tugged at his shirt, he let me know that he wanted me too.

Breaking our kiss to take off his shirt, I longed for its return. Pulling at my shirt when his was off, I removed mine. Straddling me when he was done, he looked down at me with hunger.

He couldn't take his eyes off my body. Pushing his fingers across the ripples on my chest, he moaned. It made my cock twitch. He was so beautiful and delicate. He was at once, a bird I wanted to protect and a boy I wanted to fuck.

And I did want to fuck him. I had wanted to for a long time. I couldn't have admitted it before, not even to myself. But it was always there, drawing me back to him.

Wrapping my large hands around his chest, I held him. I had never touched my best friend like this before. He was smaller than I thought he would be. Sliding my hand down to his waist, he was smaller still.

God, did I love holding him. It was almost as much as what he did next. Leaning forward, he took my flesh between his teeth. Tugging lightly, he laid his body on top of mine. He had done it to get into my pants. With them open, he kissed a path down my torso, through the valley of my abs, and onto my underwear's waistband.

With only a thin cloth between him and my hard cock, he pressed his cheek against it. Wiping my bulge across his face, his bottom lip rode the raised length of it.

Ending with a kiss on the top of my head, he looked up my body into my eyes.

"Yes," I said, giving him permission to take my cock into his mouth.

Pulling off my jeans and underwear, that was what he did. With both of his small hands wrapped around me, he plunged my head into his mouth. It was Merri who was doing this. It was amazing. And as the tip of his tongue traced the bottom of my ridge, I held his head and threw mine back.

This felt better than anything I had felt in my life. What topped it off was that it was Merri's mouth doing it. About to lose control thinking about it, I gripped the back of his head and pulled him off me.

I needed him. I wanted to be inside him. Sitting up and scooping him into the crook of my arm, I switched our positions. Laying him underneath me, I kissed his chest as I removed the last thing between us. With his pants and underwear lying beside us, I clutched the back of his thighs, playing with his cock with my tongue.

Merri's manhood was beautiful. I couldn't believe I was touching it. Sucking at it before moving to his balls, I bounced them on my tongue while lifting his knees to his chest. Spreading his legs, I found his hole. Pressing my forehead to his taint, the tip of my tongue found his opening.

As soon as I touched it, Merri squealed. It made me want more. Tickling and pushing, I loosened his hole. And when Merri sounded like he couldn't take anymore, I slid up his body and found his lips.

Kissing him, I lined up my cock and slowly pushed into him. He moaned. I paused before pushing harder.

"Yes," he whispered. "More."

I gave him more. Pressing harder as he winced, I thrust my hips until I entered him with a pop.

"Ahh," he yelped.

Like a deer caught in headlights, he looked into my eyes. We were thinking the same thing. After years of friendship, I was inside him. He fit me like a glove. We were perfect for each other.

Sliding in until I could go no further, I slowly retracted. Pushing back in, I needed to kiss him. I loved what we were doing and wanted him to know it. I wanted to show him all the things I couldn't say. So, sliding my arm around his back, I perched on top and made love to him.

It was sweet, comfortable, and more than anything, hot. Merri's body was perfect. His angles matched my bends. And when I could no longer be gentle, my thrusting made him moan in a way that gripped my soul.

"Yes. Yes!" he cried.

Fucking him harder and harder, I could see his toes curl. He was fighting to hold back. That sent a tingle up my legs to my balls. Quickly, I was struggling. I wanted this to last forever. But when Merri exploded without either of us touching his dick, I came inside him. Flowing into him like a river, my twitching didn't stop.

Tightly gripping his body, eventually, I released him. With his legs lowering around me, I was still inside him. I didn't want to leave him until I had to. And eventually, when I shrank out of him, I climbed up beside him and pulled him into my arms.

There was so much I wanted to say, but didn't. He had to know how I felt about him, though, didn't he? He must have. Merri meant everything to me. Couldn't he understand that I never wanted this to end?

Chapter 13

Merri

No, no, no, no, no. I mean, yes. A hard yes. But no.

I didn't mean for this to happen. Did I want this to happen? Of course. I've been wanting this from the day I met him. But this was going to ruin everything.

I love Claude. And I don't mean in the way that his incredibly chiseled body makes me feel. And that's saying a lot considering he has those 'V' shaped side muscles that are constantly pointing to his surprisingly large dick.

No. I love him in the way that someone does when they want the person to be in their life until they die. I didn't need to have sex.

Don't get me wrong, feeling him push into me is going to be what I spank off to for the next few years. It was better than anything I could have dreamed of. But there was more to Claude than what he could do with his body. And that was the part of him that I was in love with.

If I could take back everything that just happened I would. I would need a lobotomy for that, because there was no way I would forget this. But if that was the trade-off to have him as a friend forever, I would do it.

Still, the feeling of him holding me under the stars was incredible. I could hear the waves lightly lapping at the shore. The moonlight cast a faint shadow over everything. And despite there being a cool ocean breeze, his warm body enveloped me like a blanket.

I could enjoy this for at least a few more minutes before I had to bring this to an end. Wait, did I have to bring this to an end? Yes. Yes, I definitely had to bring this to an end.

"We should probably go," I told him – like a crazy person.

When Claude spoke, he sounded confused.

"Okay."

Was he now regretting what he did and rethinking ever having come to Florida? Probably. Claude was straight. Or, at least mostly straight. There was no way what had happened was anything more than an experiment. And whereas I would have loved to be that experiment while we were in university, after experiencing life without him for two years, I no longer wanted to risk it.

"Did you not want to go?" I asked, nervously wondering if this was where I was going to lose him.

"No, we should go," he said with more resolve.

When he unwrapped his arms from around me, I felt naked. More than that, I felt awkward and cold. As we both found our clothes and shook the sand out of them, I peeked over at Claude. He looked as stoic as ever. How did he make stoic look so hot? It was enough to make me hard again.

But no, I couldn't go there. Not tonight. Not ever again. And I had to spend whatever time he gave me before disappearing again making up for what just happened.

Dressed and packed, we headed back up the beach and into the woods.

"You didn't happen to bring a flashlight, did you?" He asked me as we entered the darkness.

"I brought candles," I reminded him, hoping it would excuse my obvious oversight.

"I liked the candles. It was a good choice," he said cheerfully, making me feel a little better.

Not wanting to relight the candles for fear of having to face what I had done, we slowly found our way to the wooden path and back to our car.

"You chose a good spot. That was nice. Thanks," he said in a tone that told me that he was going to pretend we hadn't done what we had.

That was good. It would give me more time before he couldn't pretend anymore and he ran off, never speaking to me again.

With the drive back to my place being incredibly quiet, I had a lot of time to think. Did I say think? I meant panic about every breath he took that wasn't perfectly calm and measured. Perhaps if we could get through tonight without the shit hitting the fan, I could salvage this.

"I guess we should go to bed," he said as we stood in my living room. "Back to practice tomorrow?"

"Yep, back to the grind… I mean practice," I said, hearing what I had said. "We're going back to practice tomorrow… our schedule."

It was official, I had forgotten how to speak.

"Okay. Sounds good."

Of course it sounded good to him. It would mean that he wouldn't have to deal with what we just did. He could ignore it. I mean, not that it was a bad thing. As soon as he could forget it, we could get back to rebuilding our relationship.

"Soooo…," Claude said, looking at the couch.

"It's not that comfortable, is it?" I admitted, woefully.

"It's fine. It's more comfortable than a few beds I've slept on. It's just small."

"I mean, you could sleep in my bed if you want. But, you should know that I snore."

"I'm the one who informed you of that during one of the many times we shared a tent."

"That's right! So, it shouldn't be a problem then," I said, both sweating and getting aroused.

"If you don't want me to…"

"No, no. It's not that. It's just…" I closed my eyes, making what I had to say easier. "I don't think we should do what we did, again."

Claude looked at me, confused.

"Of course. Right." He paused. "But, just so we're both clear, why not?"

How did I explain to him that I was terrified that he would get tired of my ass and leave?

"You came here to prepare for the showcase. I think we should both focus on that. You're only going to get one shot and I want this for you. It will be like how a boxer doesn't have sex before a fight."

"A boxer. Right," he said, apprehensively.

I desperately wanted to change the topic.

"Did you want to take a shower first?" I asked him.

"No, you can go first. I know how long I take in there," he said, no longer looking at me.

Leaving him and practically running to the bathroom, I closed the door behind me and rested my forehead on it. What was I doing? Had I just assumed that he would want to have sex with me again? And did I invite him into my bed?

I was trying to be a good guy. How was I supposed to do that with him lying next to me half-naked every night?

Taking the coldest shower I could, I left the bathroom, finding him lost in thought on the couch.

"All yours," I said, crossing the hallway to my room.

Within, I wasn't sure what to do. Did I close the door to put on underwear? He had already seen me naked. Hell, he had me in his mouth, and now we would be sleeping in the same bed.

Dropping my towel with the door open, I searched for a pair of underwear from my drawer. Looking back when I felt someone staring at me, I saw Claude enter the bathroom. This was going to be awkward, and it was all my fault.

I hadn't bought a picnic basket by mistake. He had asked me if my suggested night off would be a date. Did I want it to be a date? Of course, I did. But I thought it would be like one of my silly closet-case dates I would take him on in school. Like then, I thought it would be enough to further my fantasy that we were dating without actually ruining things.

But that was not what happened. I blame the alcohol. Or, the fireworks. Could it have been the candles?

Whatever it was, it made it the most romantic night of my life. I was just a weak gay boy. What resistance did I have to a moment like that?

Searching for my best pair of underwear, I put them on and looked around. Doing some quick straightening up, I made the bed and got into it.

There was no way I was going to be able to decide on what our bedroom rules would be. So, turning off the lights, I abdicated the responsibility. I was going to pretend to be asleep when he entered. That way I wouldn't have to know what I was doing, or look at his incredible body again. There was only so much I could resist.

As always, Claude took forever to shower. What did he do in there? Whatever it was, it had been long enough to legitimately claim to no longer be awake.

Lying in the darkness, I followed the sound of him around the room. As if he was staring at me, realizing I was asleep, he then quietly exited the room. Had he changed his mind about sharing my bed?

Turns out, he hadn't. He was just getting his stuff. And when I heard his towel hit the floor telling me he was naked, I did what I shouldn't have. I peeked.

Yep, he was just as hot as I remembered… And now my dick was hard again. Rock hard. Great! How was I supposed to fall asleep now?

With my eyes closed, I again followed the sound of him around the room. He did things I couldn't recognize until he gently got into bed. With him settled, I could feel him inches from me. My heart thumped so hard I could hear it. It was so loud I was sure he could as well.

If he did, he didn't say anything. He just laid there, I assume being oblivious and gorgeous. How had I gotten myself into this situation? Being this close to him without being able to touch him was torture. I was never going to sleep again.

After an hour lying there, traumatized, I was about to give up. Concluding that I would live the rest of my life awake, I rolled onto my side.

My movement must have woken him because as soon as I moved, he moved too. And when he moved, it was towards me. More precisely, it was with his chest touching my back and his arm wrapped around me. Did he know he was doing this? Should I do something to get him off of me so he had fewer things to regret in the morning?

I was about to wiggle to wake him up again when instead, I moved my hand to touch his. As our fingers met, his lightly tightened onto mine, and I immediately fell asleep.

The next morning, remembering what Claude and I had done the night before, my eyes popped open. It was late. Looking around expecting to find Claude, he wasn't there. Nor was his stuff.

I was sure I had heard him move it into the bedroom last night. But this morning it was gone. He was gone. As I had thought, what we had done had been too much for him. He had disappeared on me again.

Scrambling out of bed as panic set in, I rushed into the living room. It looked like it had before he had moved in, empty. He had left me. We had had sex and it had ruined everything.

Spiraling into despair, tears welled in my eyes. I couldn't take this. Why did I keep messing things up? I was the screw-up Papa always treated me as. I didn't deserve to be loved. I wasn't worthy of anything.

That was when I heard a key enter the lock and the door open. I swung around to find a sweaty Claude entering the apartment. Taking one look at me, he said,

"What's wrong? Why are you crying?"

I quickly wiped my tears away.

"What are you talking about? I always cry in the mornings."

"No. You always jack off in the mornings," he said, correcting me as he got a glass of water.

"That was one time!"

He gave me a disbelieving look.

"It was a couple of times. I was in the midst of going through a lot of stress."

"We were on a camping trip at Mount Rainier."

"Oh, you were talking about then. Well, that was because I didn't think you were awake."

"I wasn't until you started jacking off."

To my humiliation, he began to imitate me whimpering as I hid an orgasm.

"Ah, ah."

"Shut up!" I protested. "And where were you just now?" I asked, changing the subject.

"I've decided to go back to doing my morning runs. It feels good."

"Where's your stuff?"

"I put everything away. I hope you don't mind; I claimed a part of your closet and drawers. I don't have a lot, so you still have plenty of room."

"No, that's fine," I said, overwhelmed with relief. "I probably should have offered it to you before instead of making you live out of your bag."

"You probably should have," he said, teasing me on the way to the bathroom. "I'm taking a shower."

"I'll see you tomorrow," I said, teasing him back.

To my surprise, Claude's next workout was the best yet. He had shaved a full second and a half off his 50-yard dash, which was huge. And his cross-field passes were perfectly on point.

"Do you know what the difference is?" He asked me after I showed him the stats.

"Your morning run?" I asked, hoping he would say it was having his dick in my ass.

"Yeah, that's it," he replied, looking away disappointed.

What had he wanted me to say? 'Take all of your stuff and leave my apartment.' Because that was what I might as well have said if I suggested that it was the sex.

No, I wanted us to get back to what we had. I've accepted that things will never be exactly the same. And once he shows everyone what he can do at the showcase, he'll end up on some team halfway across the country.

But if during this summer we rebuilt our connection, maybe this time we'd stay in contact. Maybe we'd even watch each other's kids grow up. Did I want all of his babies to be mine? Obviously. But if I had to choose one, I knew which one I'd pick.

Over the following weeks, Claude's stats got better and better. It turns out that we really had unlocked something within him. On top of that, things between us had never been better.

Every night I fell asleep wrapped in his strong arms. Initially, he wouldn't hold me until we had been in bed long enough to believe that he was asleep. But too frustrated to wait it out one night, as soon as I turned off the lights, I backed into him. Still not doing it, I kept bumping him with my butt until he got the picture.

I'm sure he held me just to stop me from annoying him. But I was tired. I wanted to go to sleep. And that didn't happen until I was buried in his arms with his scent all over me. What else was I supposed to do?

It was pretty soon after that something else happened. I found something in the bathroom after one of his insanely long showers. On the fogged-up mirror, there was a drawing of someone lying in bed with a speech bubble next to him. In it was written, 'Fart'.

Was he telling me that I farted in my sleep? How dare he? To think, I gave up jacking off in the mornings for of him. Rude! This required a response. But what?

I didn't say anything about it when I left the bathroom. Instead, I plotted. What could I draw on the mirror to get back at him? Could I draw something that pointed out how annoyingly perfect his body was?

I guess I could. But it wasn't the right tone. And maybe that just came to mind because I was brainstorming while watching him go through practice drills with his shirt off.

Damn, was he hot. He had to know what being forced to watch him shirtless was doing to me, didn't he? He was such a bastard. A very hot, very ripped bastard.

It was then that it hit me. I knew what I was going to draw. But, how and when?

I could probably do something that appeared when the mirror fogged up from his crazy long shower. So, what could I use so that the drawing didn't fog up? There was stuff for that, wasn't there? I had to do some research.

"Can't be bothered to pay attention today?" Claude asked me when he caught me on my phone instead of timing his sprints.

"Sorry, something important came up," I told him, putting my phone away.

"Was it about whether or not they're gonna fire you?"

"No. And I don't think they are. Think about it. How can you fire the gay guy after he calls you out for making derogatory comments in front of others? That's a lawsuit waiting to happen. I might now have more job security than Papa does," I said with a chuckle.

Claude laughed. "You're right. You might. So what was it?" He asked, referring to me being on my phone.

"Nothing," I told him. "It was just something personal."

"Oh. Okay," he replied, seeming a little hurt.

Yeah, whatever. He brought this on himself. He would rue the day he made fun of me for farting in my sleep. And that day was coming soon.

After practice and dinner, I snuck off while he was taking his evening shower. Rushing to the auto parts store, I picked up a bottle of the defogger you put on windshields.

"Where were you?" He asked from the couch when I got back.

"Doing drugs," I told him in a panic.

"Cultivating a new addiction?"

"People have been raving about heroin. I thought I would give it a shot."

"What did you think?" He asked, returning to his book.

"It's fine. But you meet the most interesting people at the opium dens," I said, headed to the bathroom.

"I didn't know they had opium dens in Pensacola."

"Are you kidding? The opium dens here are world-class. You come for the heroin, you stay for the addictive appetizers."

"I see," he said, having lost interest in our conversation.

With the bathroom door closed, I pulled out the bottle and my phone. I was going to have to figure out how to draw this.

"You okay in there?" he asked after what turned out to be thirty minutes.

"Yeah. It's just the heroin."

"It really clogs you up, huh?"

"Exactly. I'll be out in a minute."

He had to know something was up, didn't he? He had to. Luckily, I was almost done.

Part of the problem was that I didn't have a misty mirror to draw in. I had to look at the smears I was making at weird angles to know what it looked like. Then when I screwed up, I had to start over.

After all of this work, he better appreciate the masterpiece I created. You could never find a better illustration of a man with his head up his ass drawn on a mirror using defogger fluid if you tried.

"Done," I told him when I left the bathroom. Closing the door behind me—hoping he wouldn't see it until after his morning run—I said, "I wouldn't go in there if I were you."

"I'm not sure heroin agrees with you."

"It doesn't. But you never know until you try, right?"

"I guess. Are we going to bed?"

"Sure," I told him, positive that I was too excited to sleep.

Getting into bed, my mind raced thinking about what he would say when he saw it. I almost got back up to play video games to wind down. But then he wrapped his arms around me and I was out. Turns out that Claude was the only drug I needed.

Waking up the next morning and finding him gone, I remembered my work of art and scurried out of bed. Having gotten up late, I had missed his run. He was already in the shower.

Not knowing what to do with myself, I headed towards the kitchen before changing my mind and hurrying back to bed. I wanted to be as casual as possible when he got out. What was more casual than still being asleep?

"You gonna sleep forever?" He asked me when he returned to the bedroom in a towel.

"Huh? Sorry, I was sleeping."

"I saw that," he told me as he dropped his towel and stood naked in front of me... that bastard.

Immediately aroused, I now definitely couldn't get out of bed.

"I was thinking that we could practice a few intentional fumble plays today," he said, slowly walking around instead of getting dressed.

"They wouldn't work as well in NFL play as they did in Division II."

"Maybe not. But it's good to have a few just in case," he said, turning around and presenting me with his perfectly rounded, half-moon ass.

"Whatever you want."

And by that, I meant that he could have anything he wanted. When he looked like that, I was ice cream in his hot hands. It was a good thing he got dressed. I was five seconds away from throwing myself at him; friendship be damned.

When he was fully clothed, and I could again stand, I got out of bed and headed into the bathroom. Expecting to see my masterpiece in the fogged mirror, I didn't. I had drawn a man with his head up his ass in two parts. On the right side of the mirror, I had drawn a naked ass where the person was leaning forward with their torso cut off by the edge of the glass. On the left, I had drawn the continued torso with shoulders and arms butt up to the ass cheeks. Like I said, it was a work of art.

But that wasn't what I found this morning. There was still a naked ass on the right side of the mirror. However, on the left was the picture of a head that kind of resembled mine. And it was kissing the naked ass.

Was that why he was walking around the bedroom naked? And why he clearly showed me his butt? Was he telling me to kiss his ass?

Oh, this was on. That night I drew a picture of a guy with his head stuck up a donkey's butt. You know, in case he missed the head up his ass reference the first time. Then when I got into the bathroom after him, I found the same donkey, but this time the guy was lying beneath him with the donkey's extended member fed into his mouth.

"What the...?"

This image was straight-up pornography. Yet, somehow still impressive. How did he get so much detail on a foggy mirror? It was crazy. I was clearly going to have to step up my game.

That night, redrawing the donkey, I extended its dick to circle back around into its own ass. In other words, I was telling him to fuck himself. Let's see him beat that.

He did. He drew a naked guy that miraculously resembled him, fucking a guy that resembled me. Was he telling me, "Fuck you"?

Oh, that was good... and super hot. Relieving myself to the thought of it, I held back my moans when I came. I didn't want to give him the satisfaction of knowing he had made me cum. He didn't deserve it. And to be honest, I was a little mad at him.

Was it fair? No, it wasn't. But neither was torturing me with the thought of having sex with him. Didn't he understand how hard this was for me?

Of course, I wanted to have sex with him. Of course, I wanted to feel his large hands around my waist as he manhandled me like a ragdoll.

Spreading my legs apart with his feet, he would force my naked torso forward, spreading my cheeks. With my hands against the wall, he would take hold of his oversized cock and brush it against my hole. He would tease me until he knew I couldn't take it anymore.

Then, when my knees threatened to crumble from lust, he would push into me. Throwing my head back from the painful pleasure, he would stick his finger in my mouth. Caught on his hook, he would fuck me. I wouldn't be able to do anything about it.

Drilled into the wall, I would groan until my legs shook. He would know just how long to hold on until cumming. Then, when he did, it would be an explosion. I would cum along with him. And still unable to take my palms off the wall, I would cover the floor like an animal.

Needing to relieve myself for the second time thanks to Claude's mirror drawing, I finished my shower and returned to the living room defeated. Staring at him, he clearly had no idea what he did to me. That was probably my fault. When I told him how I felt, it was always in the past tense. That was in part because I didn't want to make him feel uncomfortable. But was that the only reason?

After driving my best friend away and failing to make things work with Jason, it was safe to say that I had issues. Was it wrong not to want to be hurt again? How far back did my hurt go? I know it didn't help seeing the disappointment on my father's face when he realized I was different. He even acted differently toward me after that.

Part of the reason I had started helping Papa with football was to show him that I wasn't a disappointment. I could be the child he wanted. Maybe I was still trying to be that for my father, but luckily enough, somewhere along the way, I began to enjoy what I did.

I liked guys that looked like Claude, and where could I find that type? On a football field.

On top of that, I enjoyed helping players figure things out. I liked being a part of a team. I didn't have the build to withstand a 200 lb man running at me at full speed. But I could come up with plays that helped players win the game.

Football and I were the perfect combination. What started out as a way to prove something to my father turned into something I liked doing. But that didn't take away the pain that got me into it. Rejection hurt, whether it was from Papa, the guys on the team, or my best friend.

I wanted to be with Claude. I wanted to spend the rest of my life with him. But what I wanted more was for him not to leave me again. And if I had to choose, I would choose a guaranteed little of what I liked, over risking it all for what I truly wanted.

"Have you ever been to a pride festival?" I asked him over dinner that night.

"No. Why would I?" Claude asked sincerely.

"I don't know. You can't think of any reason?" I asked suggestively.

"I'm not gay," Claude said defensively.

"I didn't say you were."

"You were implying it."

"I was implying it because," I stopped myself before reminding him of when he had his dick in my ass. "Why don't you tell me what you are?"

"What do you mean?"

"I mean, how do you identify?"

"I don't."

"Oh, are you one of those 'I don't believe in labels' types?" I asked dismissively.

"Is there something wrong with that?"

"No. It's fine. I just think it's convenient. That's all."

"Convenient, how?"

"You know, if you don't want to admit to who you are or be thought of as 'one of those people', you can just say, 'I don't believe in labels'. That way you get all of the benefits of the struggle without having to claim any of the bad stuff."

"I see," he said, trying to hide being upset.

This annoyed me.

"Okay, Claude, I know your whole thing is not talking about stuff, but let's not right now."

"We should probably leave," he said, referring to the restaurant.

"No. We should stay here and talk about this."

Claude stared into my eyes, withdrew cash, placed it on the table, and left. He was upset, so of course, I ran after him.

"So, you're just gonna walk away?" I asked as I followed him down the street. "After everything that's gone on between us, you still can't have a simple conversation about how you feel about me?"

Claude swung around angrily.

"You know how I feel about you?"

"How? You never talk about it."

"You know what we did. Do you think I just do that with anybody?"

"How would I know? You've never told me. You don't tell me anything. 'No labels' isn't just your identity. It's your way of life."

"Well, I'm sorry I'm such a pain in your ass. If you want me to, I'll go."

"What the fuck, Claude? I ask you to tell me something about yourself, and you threaten to leave me?"

"I wasn't threatening to leave you," Claude insisted.

"Well, it sure sounded like it from here," I said, shaking from his threat.

Claude paused and looked at me. I was trembling. I wished I was strong enough not to, but I was. Feeling naked in front of him, I was raw. If he had left me there, I would have been destroyed. I knew it. There were only so many blows I could take.

As he wavered, my heart broke. I was about to fall to my knees when his large, strong arms wrapped around me.

"I don't want to leave you," he whispered into my ear. "I never did. I never want to again."

"Then why did you?" I asked with tears soaking his shirt.

"I don't know. What you said hurt so much."

"I'm so sorry I said that, Claude."

"I know you are."

"Then, why won't you forgive me?"

Claude remained silent.

"Why won't you, Claude?"

"I don't know. But it doesn't mean I don't want to be here."

"I just want you to open up to me."

"I'm trying, Merri. I really am."

"I know. I can see it. You just really suck at it."

Claude laughed. "I do. I really do."

I pulled away, looking up at him.

"But you don't always have to suck at it. For example, share one thing with me now."

"What do you want to know?"

"What is your actual identity? I know you don't like to think about it. But make me believe that this thing between us isn't just in my head."

Claude looked at me painfully.

"Please, Claude. If I mean anything to you…"

"You do," he said, cutting me off.

"Then what?"

"I thought you could see it. I'm here."

"But I need to hear it. From you," I said, touching his chest. "So please, what are you?"

Claude thought about my question. Taking a deep breath, he said,

"Well, I'm not straight. I think that ship has sailed."

"Okay."

"I don't think I'm gay," he said apprehensively.

"What makes you think you're not?"

"Women. Have you seen them?"

"I have. What's your point?"

"Right. Gay. My point is that for most of my life, I liked women."

"Have you ever been with a woman?" I asked, not knowing how I would feel hearing that he had.

"Have you?" he countered.

"You know I have."

"And now you're gay. So, what does having been with a woman prove?"

"Nothing, I guess. But it would at least tell me what you're thinking."

"Fine. I have been with women."

I thought about that, letting it process.

"When?" I challenged when it had.

"During university."

"When?" I asked more doubtfully.

"Jodi and I," he explained.

I searched my memory for who this was.

"Wait, you were having sex with Jodi?"

"Yeah," he admitted shyly.

"Seriously?"

"Why are you so surprised by that?"

"Because in three years of seeing you every day, you never told me that."

"Like I said, why are you so surprised by that?"

I stared at him shocked and then laughed.

"You really don't share stuff, do you?"

"I have a problem," he conceded.

"So, when did it start?"

"Freshman year."

"Where'd you meet?"

"It was at a fraternity party. You took off with some girl, and I went home with Jodi."

"What?" I asked, stunned and amused.

"Yeah."

"And you hooked up more than just then?"

"She was trying to get into medical school and would text me whenever she needed to blow off steam. There was a lot of steam."

"But you two never dated?"

"No."

"Why not? She was cute." I paused. "Actually, she looked a lot like me."

"I have a type."

"Wait, I'm your type. What's your type?"

"Pushy. Annoying. Asks too many questions."

I laughed.

"Okay, I know that isn't true. Jodi was the most serious person I've ever met. I remember when you introduced us. She was basically a blonde version of you. Having sex with her had to be as fun as doing taxes."

"She was actually pretty wild. Sometimes I could barely keep up."

"Huh! I would never have guessed. It's always the quiet ones. So, about me being your type," I asked playfully.

Claude laughed.

"What about it?"

"Say more."

He chuckled.

"Like what?"

"Anything," I told him.

Claude relaxed, took my hands in his, and looked up in thought.

"Well, I like delicate hands."

"I don't have delicate hands," I said self-consciously.

"And I like your petite frame," he said, smiling at me.

"I'm not 'petite'," I objected.

"And I like how even when I try to give you a compliment, you reject it, making me feel like I haven't."

I caught myself.

"I guess I'm as good at receiving them as you are at giving them. But couldn't you like my manly demeanor?"

"If you had one, sure," he said with a smirk.

"Okay, now you're just being mean."

Claude joyfully transferred his hands from mine to my waist.

"I just like you for who you are, Merri. Can't you accept that?"

"You're right, Claude. Thank you. I should just accept myself for who I am."

"You should. Because what you are is wonderful. And it doesn't matter if you have hands like a marionette or a bird-like feminine frame, I still like you."

I stared at his grinning face with daggers in my eyes. Pulling away and walking off, I said,

"You know what, go back to Tennessee. No one wants you here. Goodbye."

Beside himself with amusement, he followed, asking, "What? Was it something I said?"

"Bye."

"No. Tell me. Did I say something wrong?"

"Goodbye," I repeated, secretly elated to hear him follow me.

As annoying as he could be, maybe he wasn't actually going to leave me again. And although it was my greatest fear, maybe I could trust him to be there for me after all.

Arriving back at my place unsure if I should forgive him for the horribly true things he had said, I was about to when my phone rang. Seeing me staring at the caller ID strangely, Claude asked,

"Who is it?"

"My ex, Jason."

"Isn't he the guy organizing the showcase?"

"Yeah," I said, answering the phone with a bad feeling. "Hey, Jason. What's going on?"

"I don't know how to say this, so I'm just going to get to the point."

"Okay."

"Your friend can't come to the showcase."

My heart sank. Feeling the cold chill as the blood rushed from my face, I asked,

"Why not?"

"Because my therapist says that he thinks it's unhealthy for me to keep doing favors for you considering the way you've treated me. And, frankly, I agree."

I panicked.

"But that's not what's happening. You invited him because you saw his stats, remember? He's good. And I've been working with him all summer. He's better than he's ever been."

"I'm sorry, Merri. You acted the way you did when we were together because you thought it was what was best for you. Now, it's my turn."

"You can't do this."

"Because this is something that affects you instead of just me?" Jason asked bitterly.

"No. Why would you say that? I'm talking about Claude. He's worked hard for this."

"What's going on?" Claude asked, hearing my pleas.

"I'm assuming Claude is your boyfriend now?" Jason inquired.

I froze.

"I wouldn't say that," I said, second-guessing what I was saying.

"Well, whoever he is, I don't feel it's healthy for me to help you be with someone else. You hurt me. I'm mad at you. And I have the right to act on it, just like you had the right to treat me like I didn't matter."

"But, Jason…"

"I'm not changing my mind. I'm just calling you so you didn't have to read it in a text. Good luck with everything, and I hope you end up with someone who treats you exactly how you treated me. Bye, Merri."

"But…" I said, right before the line went dead.

I lowered the phone, stunned.

"Merri, what's going on?" Claude asked, worried.

I turned to him, barely able to breathe.

"I think I screwed things up again."

"What happened?"

"Jason just withdrew your invitation to the showcase."

"What does that mean?"

"I don't know."

"So, I've been practicing all summer for nothing?"

I stared at him without an answer.

"I don't get it. Why did he change his mind?"

"Because I was a terrible boyfriend," I admitted. "He thinks I have feelings for you, and he's doing this to hurt me."

Claude backed into the couch and fell onto it. Closing his eyes, he put his hands on his forehead, trying to fight off his frustration.

"I'm sorry, Claude. I'm so sorry."

"What do we do now?"

"I don't know."

"Do I just leave?"

"No!" I said louder than I had intended. "I mean, I can think of something. I'm not going to let you down. I'll figure a way out of this."

We didn't say much more to each other for the rest of the night. Lying in bed, he didn't hold me. He had every night since we had begun sleeping together, but not tonight.

I didn't sleep at all. Instead, I spiraled, thinking about what I could possibly do. By morning, I had something. It was a long shot, but it was a chance.

As soon as I heard him stir, I presented it to him.

"You have to take me to this year's Hall of Fame game," I informed him.

Claude's tired eyes fought to focus on me.

"I know what all of those words mean. Yet I have no idea what you're talking about," Claude replied in his froggy morning voice.

"You are familiar with the Hall of Fame game, right?"

"Yeah, it's the pre-season game they play on the weekend of the NFL Hall of Fame ceremony."

"Right. And this year one of the players being inducted is someone who played for the Cougars before Papa got there. That means that the Cougars are going to have to play the Hall of Fame game. And since I haven't been fired yet, it means I will have to attend and go to the ceremonies. You have to come with me."

"I'm not sure that's a good idea," Claude said hesitantly.

"What? Scared that if people see you with me, they'll think you're gay? Instead of, 'I'm too masculine to have a label,' or however you identify?" I asked, exhausted from lack of sleep.

"No, of course not." Claude perched himself on his elbow to look at me. "Do you think I give a shit about what people think I am?"

"Yeah, I do. If you didn't, you would have given me some reassurance that I wasn't barking up the wrong tree by letting myself feel something for you."

"Merri, you're not barking up the wrong tree. Where is this coming from?"

"I just…" I caught myself and got back on course. "Look, you have to come with me to the Hall of Fame game because there will be a lot of agents there. If I can present you to them in the right way, we can get another invite to the showcase."

Claude looked at me speechless, then shook his head, reversing course. "I need to go back to something. Why would you think you're barking up the wrong tree?"

"Why would you say that going with me was a bad idea? You didn't even take a second. It was like you didn't want to be seen with me."

"Merri, I didn't think it was a good idea because you keep doing these things that make me think that I matter to you, but when I ask you to do something that proves it, you make me feel like garbage for it."

"What are you talking about?" I asked confused.

"I kissed you, and then you said you didn't want to talk about it. We had a really good time on the beach and then you immediately said that we should act like it didn't happen. You know, I used to think that I was the one preventing anything from happening between us. But I'm not the one running from it. You are.

"And now you want me to attend this thing with you? I know you're saying it's just for me, to help me. But it feels like more. It's a fancy event with all of your coworkers and everyone in the industry that you respect. Whatever else it is, it sure feels like a date. But what are you going to tell me when it's done? That we should pretend the Hall of Fame doesn't exist?"

I stared at Claude, caught off guard. "I don't understand. Would you want this to be a date?"

"Merri, I have wanted everything we've been doing to be a date. You know all those times when I've passed you the ball in practice? Consider that foreplay."

"I didn't realize you felt like that."

Claude calmed. "That might be because I'm not always great at sharing what I'm thinking. But I am now."

I smiled. "Yes, you are. But, what if people see you at the event and they assume you're gay. That might make it a lot harder to get on a team."

"Then fuck football. If football doesn't want me, I don't want it. I would choose you any day over a sport that doesn't want me. You're what matters to me, Merri. Football's just a game."

"That's really sweet."

"I don't know why you keep being surprised by that. I'm a sweet guy," he said emphatically.

I laughed.

"I guess you are," I said, staring up at the man I wanted to kiss.

"I'm glad you're finally realizing this."

"I am. And now you're my date for the Hall of Fame game," I said flirtatiously.

"It's about time," Claude joked, making me laugh.

"But we still need to get you into the showcase. And for that, we need to find you an agent."

"What does that entail?"

"If we can, we should create a reel of your best plays from university. I can compile your stats. I think I already have them. And, I know you don't like it, but you're going to have to help me sell you to the agents."

"What do you mean?" Claude asked, uneasy.

"I mean you're going to have to charm them. You know, tell them why you think you deserve this. Sell yourself."

If it wasn't for Claude's always cool demeanor, I would have sworn that he was panicking.

"I…" He began. "No."

"What do you mean, no?"

"No. I'm… No."

"Claude, you have to do this."

"I don't have to do anything."

He jumped out of bed.

"I didn't want this. You came and presented this to me like it was a done deal. But things keep changing."

"I know, I'm sorry. But we can still get it. It's just one more thing. After this…"

He cut me off.

"What? It'll be something else?"

Claude turned away and got dressed.

"This is the last thing. I promise."

"I don't want this anymore."

"Want what?" I asked, feeling a knot grow in my stomach.

"Any of this. I don't want any of it!" He said, as if realizing it for the first time.

"Where are you going?" I asked when I saw him filling his travel bag.

He turned to me.

"I don't want this, Merri. I never did. You sold me something that wasn't real. And I don't want it anymore."

"So you're just gonna go?" I asked, watching him collect his stuff. "Go where?"

"Home. Where I should have been. Where I should have never left."

A cold sweat covered me. This was my nightmare.

"I don't understand. What did I do?"

"I don't know, Merri. Why don't you tell me what you did?"

"I don't know. Tell me what I did," I said, rushing to my feet and following him out of the room. "Please tell me what I did."

With his bag packed, he turned to me coldly.

"If you don't know, I don't know what to tell you."

"Please don't go, Claude. I'm begging you, don't go," I said as tears filled my eyes.

That didn't stop him. Marching towards the door, he was about to walk out when he pulled something from his bag.

"Here, you can have this. I won't be needing it anymore."

I took the flat package from him and froze with it in my hands.

"Bye, Merri."

"You're just gonna go?"

He looked back at me. Then, without another word, he left.

I stood staring at the door, stunned. What had just happened? I didn't understand.

Turning to the package he had given me, I searched it, looking for answers. Inside was a card and a large picture frame. Opening the card, it read: 'For your first day back at work. You got this. I believe in you. I always have. And now you have something for your wall. ;)'

Flipping over the picture frame, I found a collage of our life together. On the top left was a picture from football practice our freshman year. Below that were pictures from our camping trips. On the right were parties where we were being silly. And in the center was from the 4th of July, the night we made love.

Staring at it, I cried. What had I just done? Had I finally ruined things forever?

Chapter 14

Claude

I couldn't do it. It was too much. How many times could I push past what felt comfortable and keep going?

I had overextended myself. I didn't want this anymore. There were only so many ways I could open myself up for Merri. But the thought of selling myself to a bunch of rich white guys like I was some poor black kid begging for money, was more than I could take.

I had to get away from all of this. I needed to get back around my family. So, taking a taxi to the airport, I booked the first flight available and made my way home.

"Can you pick me up?" I asked Titus as I approached the end of the bus line.

"Claude? Where are you?" He asked, surprised to hear from me.

"I'm at the bus stop. I'm back in town."

"Of course. It might be a few hours, though. I'm just about to take a group out for a tour. I have another one scheduled after that."

"That's fine, I'll call someone else."

"I could ask Lou if he can do it. Though he might need to watch the shop in case anyone arrives early."

"That's fine. Don't worry about it."

"I wish you'd given me a little more notice. I could have arranged something."

"I'll call you tonight."

"We'll catch up then."

"Definitely," I said, ending the call.

Feeling lost, I wondered how I had gotten here. I had flipped out. There was no doubt about it. But why? Had Merri's request been so crazy? It hadn't been. This was the way the world worked. Yet, I couldn't get myself to even consider it. Why was that?

Looking around at the empty streets surrounding me, I knew who would have the answer.

"Momma?"

"Claude, how are you?" She asked cheerfully.

"Not good, Momma. Can you pick me up? I'm at the airport bus stop."

"Of course, Son. What are you doing home?"

"I'll tell you later. Can you just pick me up?"

"I'll be there as soon as I can."

"Thanks, Momma," I said, ending the call and lowering my face into my hands.

Seeing Momma's car pull up forty-five minutes later was a sight for sore eyes. Grabbing my bag and getting in, she honored my silence. That lasted until we were ten minutes away from home.

"I've given you long enough. Do you care to tell me what you're doing back so soon? I have your showcase marked on the calendar. It's not for another few weeks."

"I'm not in the showcase anymore," I told her.

"You aren't? Why not?"

I considered not getting into it and then realized that if I were ever to get over what it was that had me, I was going to have to talk about it.

"Because I think I'm broken, Momma," I said, fighting to keep my tears from falling.

"Baby, you're not broken. You're the strongest young man that I know."

"I'm not, Momma. I'm screwed up. Why did you tell me that thing you did about me having to represent my race. I was only 8 years old."

Momma got serious.

"I told you it because it was true. You can't afford to pretend like things are the same for you as they are for other people. The world is too dangerous for that, especially in a state like Tennessee."

"Momma, what are you talking about? My whole life, the only racism I've experienced has been because I've gone looking for it."

"So now you're telling me that racism doesn't exist? With your many years of experience, you're tryin' tell your Momma what you think you know?"

"I'm not trying to do anything. I'm telling you what my experience has been. And I'm not saying that there aren't people out there trying to keep us down so they can stay on top. I'm not even saying that people won't say stupid things. They will. I've experienced that."

"Then, what are you saying?"

"I'm saying that we see what we are taught to look for. That's all."

"So, I guess you're telling me that the way I raised you is wrong? Is that it?"

I thought about that.

"I don't know what wrong is, Momma. I just know that the way you raised me had consequences. And now my life is one big consequence I can't get past."

"Is this about that blonde boy who was at our house?"

"His name is Merri, Momma," I said sadly.

"Then, is this about Merri?"

"Yeah. Because I think I love him. And I keep running from him, and the only thought that keeps going through my head when I do is, 'What would Momma say about me being with him?'"

"You know that I don't have a problem with you being bisexual. I wouldn't care if you were gay."

"I know. But what would that say to white people about our race? Am I just another black man seeking validation by being with someone white? And if that's true, how many more stereotypes am I?"

"Claude, my son is not a stereotype," she protested.

"Really, Momma? I'm a black man who's good at sports and only has sex with white people. How much more of a stereotype could I be?"

"Son, that's not all of who you are. You're smart and thoughtful. I would add funny, but we both know how funny black people can be," she joked.

I couldn't help but huff a laugh.

"I'm serious, Momma."

"I know, Claude. So am I. And you might be right. I may have made a mistake saying that to you at such a young age. It was what my father said to me, and you growing up without a father…"

"Another stereotype," I said, cutting her off.

"…growing up without a father, I felt I had to say it to you."

"Well, I heard it. I shaped my life around it."

"That was not the purpose of me telling you."

"Wasn't it, though? Wasn't it to get me to act like a kid everyone would be proud of?"

"But it wasn't meant to be at the expense of your happiness," she said sadly.

Pulling onto our driveway, she turned off the car.

"If what I said has made you feel like you have had to live up to unrealistic expectations, then I'm sorry. I'm sorry, son. But don't let it stop you from doing what makes you happy. If Merri makes you happy, be with him."

"It's not that simple," I said, looking down.

"Then make it that simple. Maybe I also should have told you to fight for the person you love. Because when you find someone worth keeping, you push through your own stuff to be there for him."

I thought about that as we sat silently in the car.

"Did you fight for my father? What was his name again?"

"Armand Clement," Momma said with a wistful smile.

"Right. Did you fight for him?"

"That was different."

"How so?"

"Did I ever tell you that I used to have a thing for bad boys?"

Feeling like I had asked a question too many, I shrank in my seat.

"No, you didn't. Do I want to hear this? Momma, think about everything we just talked about—about you telling me things you shouldn't—and ask yourself if this is what you need to be telling me right now."

Momma looked at me, then pretended to lock her lips and throw away the key.

"Thank you, Momma."

"And don't use anything as an excuse not to do everything you have to do to be with that little blonde boy. He was cute. If I was thirty years younger…"

"And he was straight?" I asked her.

She laughed.

"I guess you can have that one. But please, Son, don't let me be the cause of your unhappiness. It would break my heart," she said sincerely before opening her door and leaving me there to think.

Chapter 15

Merri

"Get your head in the game, Merri," Papa yelled, snapping me back to reality. "Am I gonna have to replace you?"

"No, Coach," I replied, wondering how many people had heard him.

Looking around, I realized the answer was everyone. I was screwing up again. I couldn't stop screwing up.

Claude was supposed to be here with me. Not on the sidelines of the Hall of Fame game. But, in Ohio and in the stands.

He had left me, again. Was I worth so little to everyone? Would anyone even care if I wasn't around?

I doubted my father would. I was just a burden to him at this point. I was his little gay son who made his life and job harder. I would never make him happy. What was I even doing here?

As the game came to a close with six interceptions driving our loss, I stood behind Papa as he gave the team his losing game speech. Papa emphasized that the loss was everyone's responsibility. But it was hard to win when your quarterback can't complete a pass to save his life.

Sure, he would blame the offensive line for not giving him enough time, or the receivers for fumbling his passes. But I had seen more done with less. And that quarterback's name was…

"Claude!" I said, entering my room and finding him there. "What the hell? What are you doing here? How did you get in? And why are you wearing a tuxedo?"

Claude smiled his brilliant, glowing smile.

"Those were a lot of questions."

"Then start with, 'What the hell?'"

Thinking for a second, he said, "I don't know how to respond to that."

"Seriously, Claude, what are you doing here?"

"Well, as I remember, you agreed to have me as your date for this event. Did you think I was just gonna forget about that?"

"Stop it, Claude. Tell me, what you're doing here?"

"Making a grand romantic gesture?" he asked apprehensively.

"But you left me. No explanation. No warning. You just left."

"Yeah," he said, embarrassed.

"Where'd you go?"

"To have a hard conversation."

"I see. And what was that hard conversation about?"

"About why I keep leaving you," he said humbly.

I stared at him with my mouth hanging open. Nervously, I asked,

"And why is that?"

"It's something called generational trauma."

"What's that?"

"It's when someone experiences something bad, and they teach their child how to react to it and they teach their child, and they teach their child. It's a black thing."

"As the gay son of a toxic-male father, I can tell you, that's not just a black thing."

"Maybe not," he conceded.

"Okay, so why are you here?"

"I'm here to fight for you. Or, more precisely, to fight myself for you. And I want you to know that I will continue to fight until I have you. And I get that I keep disappearing on you. And that you might not want to forgive me for it. But, I'm here. And I will keep coming back... at least until you learn to better secure your doors."

"So, you're planning on stalking me. Is that it?"

Claude bobbled his head. "Maybe with a little breaking and entering."

"Is that a black thing, too?"

He stared at me and then burst into laughter.

"After saying that, you better be planning on forgiving me."

I smiled.

"Like I could ever stay mad at you. Haven't you realized I have issues?"

"I thought we weren't supposed to talk about it."

Disarmed, I walked over to the love of my life and wrapped my arms around him.

"I thought I had lost you."

"You'll never lose me. Did you hear my speech about breaking and entering?"

"I heard it. It was very reassuring."

"You do have issues."

"I know. So do you."

"I know," Claude said, holding me tighter.

"Wait," I said, pulling away. "Why are you wearing a tuxedo?"

"A, I wanted to remind you of how hot I am, in case the breaking and entering speech didn't work."

"Check."

"B, I wanted to make you look good for the ceremony tonight. I wasn't joking about collecting my date."

I smiled, looking up at the most gorgeous man I had ever seen in my life. I loved him, wholly and completely.

"I know this wasn't why you came and is probably why you left, but if you still want to be in the showcase, I met an agent today," I said hesitantly.

Claude reacted by tensing up. Closing his eyes and taking a breath, he relaxed.

Opening his eyes, he smiled and said, "If it's someone you think I should meet, then I would love to meet them."

I couldn't express how good that made me feel. He deserved a real shot at making a team, and I wanted to do this for him. No matter what had gone on between us, I knew he loved football. I wanted him to be happy.

But tonight wouldn't be the night to introduce the two. It would be tomorrow. That was when the fancy ceremony was. That was when Claude could make everyone's jaw drop by wearing his tuxedo.

Tonight, I was going to have to leave Claude to have dinner with the team as a bonding event. We'd had a few of them since the start of mini-camp and they hadn't helped our pass completion rate. It looked like this was going to be another disappointing season for the Cougars, and the last with Papa and me.

Eating dinner and listening to the players' speeches about how great the season will be, all I could think about was Claude. I couldn't believe he was here.

There was a part of me that thought I should be upset with him for leaving again, but could I be at this point?

It's not like he was meaning to hurt me. And hadn't he come back on his own this time? Neither of us were perfect, especially me. So wasn't it enough that we were fighting to be the best versions of ourselves for each other? Considering perfection wasn't an option, could either of us ask for more than that?

Returning to my room, I could only think of one thing, sleeping in his arms. I hadn't slept well since he had left. A part of it was dealing with the heartbreak of him leaving. But the other part was that I never felt more loved and accepted than when I was being held by him.

"How was dinner?" he asked me.

"You tell me," I said, handing him a carryout container.

"Oh," he said, taking it. "I told you that I was going to grab some fast food."

"I know. But I didn't want you to miss out on the glory of experiencing a romp roast hurriedly made for 40 people."

"Oh, you're so sweet," he said sarcastically.

"I try to be."

"You should keep trying," he said, teasingly.

I laughed.

"So, how have you been?" Claude asked, putting the container on the room's desk and lying in bed.

Although there were two beds, I crawled into his and buried myself in his arms.

"Would it be too much to say that life is never as good without you?" I asked.

"It wouldn't be too much. Maybe a lot, though."

"In that case, life has been swell. I've especially liked watching Brad miss passes I know you could make."

"Sounds fun."

"What about you? How have you been?"

"Regretful. Remorseful. There's been a lot of second-guessing myself."

"Sounds fun."

"It's been a blast," he replied with sadness in his tone. "I don't mean to keep running away. It's like a knee-jerk reaction. I get this feeling like I can't breathe and all I want is space."

"Have you been working on that?" I asked hesitatively.

"When I was home, I had a few conversations with Kendall."

"Isn't he Nero's boyfriend?"

"Yeah. How did you know?"

"I met him at game night. Wasn't he a therapist or something?"

"He's studying to be."

"What did he say?"

"He said I was an idiot for not locking you down immediately."

"He sounds like a very wise man."

"He had been drinking at the time, so I'm not sure it was his best advice. But when he was sober, he told me to be kind to myself. He said I shouldn't expect more from myself than I do from others. When he said it, I realized he was a crazy person, but we're going to continue talking anyway."

"That's good. Maybe I should talk to someone."

"About what? You're perfect."

I turned around and looked at Claude, shocked. "Did you just compliment me? Like, give me a real compliment unprompted? My god, therapy's working. Are you gonna outgrow me?"

"That's the plan. That way I can trade up for a healthier, more stable person who looks just like you. Because obviously, you're my type."

I looked at him frustrated. "There he is. The man I love," I said sarcastically.

I put my head back on his chest. After a moment, in a vulnerable voice, he said, "I love you too."

Had he just said that? I panicked. When I had said it, I was joking. We always joked like that. Had he taken it seriously?

I mean, I loved him. Of course, I did. I had loved him forever. But there was a big difference between telling him that I used to be in love with him, acting like

I'm in love with him, and actually saying I love him while doing the loving.

How was I supposed to respond? Perhaps any response would have been better than how I did, which was with silence.

God damn, was I a mess. This was Claude, the man of my dreams. There was a time when I would cry at night hoping to hear what I just had. Yet, I couldn't say it back. What was wrong with me?

Luckily, Claude didn't jump out of bed and run. It seemed that my particular brand of crazy wasn't what triggered him. Thank God for that. And, if I were really quiet for the rest of the night, maybe he would let me fall asleep in his arms without reminding me of how awful I was.

That wasn't quite what happened, but what did happen wasn't bad. After what felt like forever, he asked me if I wanted to change. I told him that I was trying. But he had been talking about my clothes. That broke the tension.

Getting changed and returning to his arms, we fell asleep quickly after that. Waking to the sound of him showering after his morning run, I looked at the clock realizing I had to get going. I could only stare at his half-naked body as he got dressed for a short time today. Damn! Talk about the best part of waking up…

Hurrying into the bathroom after him, I almost missed the drawing on the mirror. I was excited to see it until I saw what it was. It was an image of two people lying with speech bubbles over them. One read, 'I love you.' The second was a series of 'Zzzzz', that bastard.

Rubbing it out without time to draw a reply, I hopped into the shower. Getting dressed and hurrying out, I told him that I would be back later to get ready for dinner. That was what I did.

Happy to see his hot body adorned in his tuxedo, I returned to the bathroom for another quick shower and found something else. Instead of there being a drawing on a fogged mirror, there was a fridge magnet stuck to the mirror's metal frame. The magnet was an image of a clown saying 'I love you' while staring down at a pickle waiting for a response.

Did I used to think that Claude was a good guy? Because I was wrong. He was a dick.

Slipping it into my palm on the way out, I made sure not to acknowledge it when I saw him again. And the guy was amazing. There was nothing about him that hinted that he had left it.

Playing along, I put on my tuxedo and got ready to head out.

"Is that James Bond?" he asked, looking at me.

"What?" I asked, clueless.

"Sorry, for a second you looked like James Bond."

Confused, I asked, "You do know what James Bond looks like, right?"

"Like the taller Hobbit from Lord of the Rings."

"No, that's... Merri," I said, realizing what he was doing.

"Right! Yeah, that's who you look like. Wait, who did I say? Anyway, should we go?"

Having had my fill of Claude, I then led my lovely date to the grand ballroom. Heads turned. And as much as I would like to believe that it was for me, there was no denying how great Claude looked tonight.

"You're like the Black James Bond. Who is this, Merri?" one of my players asked me.

"I'm his date," Claude said casually. Then, when Claude's head was turned, the player gave me his impressed-bro face with a huge thumbs up.

As degrading and dismissive as I found his reaction, I couldn't also help but feel really good. Because, yeah, I was with the hottest guy in the room, and I had seen him naked.

Forgiving Claude for his previous dickishness, I quickly relaxed and even dared to take his arm. For a guy who refused to label himself, he seemed amazingly comfortable with it. He would have made some rich old lady the perfect arm candy if I hadn't gotten to him first.

"Oh, Claude, I would like you to meet Arny. Arny, this is the quarterback I was telling you about."

Claude casually released my arm to shake Arny's hand. I could tell the stocky middle-aged man was thrown by seeing Claude escort me, but he gathered himself quickly.

"Merri, tells me you're hoping to be a part of the pre-season player showcase."

"I was hoping. Merri's been training me all summer. I think he has me right where he wants me."

"In training, that is," I added nervously.

"Yeah. His fingerprints are all over me."

"He's talking about his game. You know, his style of play."

"I see," Arny said, awkwardly. "Well, Merri has shared your college stats with me. They're very impressive. Three division titles in a row, huh? Why didn't you declare for the draft while you were eligible?"

I tensed, wondering how Claude would answer this one.

"I had issues to work through. My head wasn't in the right space for an opportunity like that," he answered sincerely.

"And now it is?"

Claude nodded. "Yeah. Merri knows how to turn my head."

Arny looked at me for clarification.

"I got nothin'," I admitted.

"Well, on the strength of your record and Merri's recommendation, I'll look into getting you a spot. If you get out there, you're not going to embarrass me, are you?" He asked with a slimy smile.

"I will give it everything I have," Claude agreed.

"He's going to do great," I assured him. "I've never seen a player like him."

"And he's seen all of me," Claude added.

"All right!" I said, unable to take any more innuendos. "I'll have him prepared and ready to go."

"You do that," Arny said before moving on to someone else.

"What was that?" I asked when we were alone.

"What was what?"

"That! He's now gonna think we slept together."

"We did sleep together."

"I remember. Believe me, I do."

"Do you?"

"It's hard to forget. And let me emphasize, hard."

Claude smiled.

"Well, I just want everyone here to know that I'm the one lucky enough to be with you and they aren't."

"That might not be as impressive as you think it is," I admitted.

"It is from where I'm standing," he said with a smirk.

I stared up at him. "You really are getting good at this complimenting thing."

"Thank you. I try," he said, content with himself. "So, who else did you want to introduce me to?"

Looking up into his milk chocolate-colored eyes, I wanted to introduce him to everyone. Everything he had said filled a hole in me I didn't know I had. I especially wanted Papa to hear him talk about me like that, but he was the last person who should have heard it.

As reckless as he was acting tonight, I had to protect him from himself. If he shined at the showcase as I thought he would, he might end up working with some of these people. I knew what it was like being gay in football. He didn't need to deal with that along with everything else he would go through.

With the business part of the evening done, I was feeling a lot lighter. I introduced Claude to a few of my more open-minded players. There was one I was pretty sure had hit on me. When we walked away from him, Claude asked,

"Is he gay?"

I laughed.

"So, you feel it too?"

"It was more about how he was looking at me like he wanted to rip off my head and fuck my throat."

"I must have missed that."

"I don't see how."

I shrugged. "Linebackers," I said dismissively.

Overall, the night had been a success. Back at our room, I watched Claude as he got undressed. God, was he getting hard to resist.

"Am I still a boxer?" he asked, referring to my suggestion that we not have sex.

That got me more than aroused. Having to cross my legs, I let the rush of heat leave my face before answering. I was sure I was turning bright red. He knew exactly what I was thinking about.

"Yes," I told him. It actually hurt to say.

When he was standing in front of me wearing only his underwear that did nothing to hide his huge erection, he pointed at my pants and said,

"Are you sure you don't need help with that?"

I was so turned on that I was threatening to pass out.

"I'm sure," I forced out. "Excuse me," I told him before getting up, heading to the bathroom, and taking things into my own hands.

"Are you sure you don't need help in there?"

Jacking myself like there was no tomorrow, I ignored him and lost myself in the memory of his scent.

"Merri?"

"Ahhh," I moaned, trying to be quiet but failing. When everything in me was out, I replied, out of breath, "No, I'm good."

"Okay."

"Just let me know."

"I will," I told him, wondering what I was doing. "Did you need to get in here next?"

"No, I'm good," he told me, walking away from the door.

Apparently, Claude had no plans on relieving himself. Instead, he pressed his outrageously hard cock against my back all night as he held me.

What was he doing to me? Didn't he know I was a weak gay boy who could only resist for so long? At least I no longer needed to try heroin. White-knuckling it through tonight was hard enough.

The strain I felt not rubbing my ass against his pole made my legs numb. Did I mention he was an asshole? Because by the time the sun rose, I was traumatized.

I did not do well without sleep. My only saving grace was that at some point he lost his erection. Did that stop my painful, aching lust? No. And because of it, I was not in a good mood the next day.

"So, we're heading back to your place?" Claude asked me as I packed.

"Yes."

"Are we going to do any more practices before the showcase?"

"No."

"Are you mad at me?"

I turned to him. I was so sexually frustrated that I felt like any moment I could snap. But somehow I calmed myself, reined it all in and said, "Dick." I thought it explained everything.

Every night after that was a nightmare. The man was torturing me. I was sure of it.

The only way I got through it was to relieve myself before we went to bed and then as soon as I got up. I wasn't sure what he was doing. But he was hard every night before he fell asleep and sometimes for a while after that.

Needless to say, I was no longer sleeping as well as I used to. And it was definitely affecting my work. When the coach caught me napping in my office, he asked if something was going on. How did I explain to him that his favorite son was torturing me with his hard cock every night?

"You look like a mess. Pull yourself together," he told me.

Didn't he understand that this was me pulled together? He didn't want to see me falling apart.

Mercifully, the player showcase was coming up quickly, and this would soon come to an end. As it approached, I often drifted off into elaborate sexual thoughts where Claude's hard cock would destroy my usually lifeless body. And when the morning finally arrived, I was sure to leave something in the bathroom for him to find.

I couldn't even pretend to sleep that night. So when he immediately returned from the bathroom holding the condom I had left, I was awake to see it.

"Now?" He asked, already hard.

"Tonight."

"Are you sure? We could do it now."

"We've waited this long."

Claude pursed his lips in frustration. He then grabbed the bedroom door and nearly tore it off the wall. It was good to see that I hadn't been the only one suffering all this time.

"Use it," I told him, fragile from horniness.

He didn't reply. But watching him at the showcase, he used it. The man was amazing.

In the 50-yard dash, he beat his personal best by two seconds. That's huge.

Then when passing, there was nowhere on the field that was safe. He threw bomb after bomb, each landing precisely. The man was an animal out there. And spotting me in the stands when the showcase was done, he eyed me like prey.

I felt scared to go to him even as I ran. My heart pounded. My knees wobbled. And when I saw him, the blood drained from my face.

I wasn't sure what happened next. All I knew was that my legs were around his waist and my back was against the wall. With his humongous hands cradling the back of my head, his tongue dug for mine.

I could barely see straight; it felt so good. And rushing to my car with my cock throbbing, we reached it just in time before he ripped off my pants and sank his cock into my hole.

"Ahh," I screamed, needing more.

What were we doing? We were in the parking structure at a football stadium.

"Yes! Yes!" I yelled, not caring who heard.

Seeming to grow in size as he mounted me, Claude didn't care either. The man fucked me like a rag doll. I could feel weeks of restraint pounded into me. He was merciless. I deserved it. And I loved every minute of it.

Somehow finding myself sprawled naked in a moving car, I became a dog in heat. Claude was driving. He was taking turns like a madman. He was speeding, but I couldn't wait.

Crawling onto the floor, I pushed my head between his legs. I was going to kill us both. I knew that. But I needed his cock in my mouth. I had waited long enough.

Pulling it out of his unzipped pants, I pushed its mushrooming tip between my lips. The taste, the smell, it was everything I dreamed it would be. This was Claude's cock, the center of all his power over me, and I had it.

Pushing it onto my tiny throat, I coughed. I was willing to choke myself on it. Luckily, I didn't have to because before I knew it, we were at my place. Carrying me like a sack, he took me from my car to our apartment. Tossing me onto the first thing he found, he stared down at me on the couch and tore off his clothes.

I became naked. I wasn't sure how. His hands were all over me. Stroking my cock, he tongued my ass.

Folding me like a pretzel, he fucked me again. I wanted it. I wanted everything he could give. My body was his to do as he willed.

Starting on the couch, we moved to the kitchen, then bathroom, and eventually the bed. My ass was worn out by the time he was done. But if he wanted, I knew I could do it again.

I had lost count of the number of times I had cum. It had been a lot. And by the time Claude was finished, he was shooting blanks. It had taken all day and night, but his barrel was empty.

It was only then, as my exhausted warrior held me, that I could say what I was always thinking. It was to a silent room. I didn't even know if he was awake.

"I love you, too," I told him, hoping he had heard. "And, I don't want you to go."

Chapter 16

Claude

Waking to the sound of a single chirp in the distance, I moved, realizing that I didn't feel great. I was sore. What had I been doing the day before? That's right, the showcase. And after that, the wildest sex of my life with the man I loved.

Carefully rolling over so as not to wake Merri, I turned, looking for him. With the early morning light streaming in through the curtains, I found him staring at me, his brow furrowed. He was never up this early. And he looked like he hadn't slept.

I was about to ask him what was going on when he said, "I think someone's trying to get a hold of you."

I heard the chirp again. It was the notification alert on my phone.

"They've been texting you for hours."

Wondering if that was why he was awake, I sat my aching body up and scanned the room. Finding nothing on the floor, I waited for another chirp. When I heard it, I realized it was coming from the living room and remembered why. God, did I love fucking Merri. When I was in him, I felt like I was home.

Feeling my dick getting hard, I got up before things got out of control. Crossing the room naked, I could feel Merri staring. I liked it when he watched me. I loved the way I looked through his eyes.

Exiting out of the hallway, I got a better picture of what we had done the day before. No wonder I was sore. Every countertop had been swept clean, and the things that had been on them were on the floor. There were broken dishes and mounds of spilt salt. It was like a hurricane had passed through the place.

Hearing the chirp again, I located my pants and retrieved my phone. In that moment before everything changed, my life was great. Hell, it was perfect. Then I read the messages and the blood rushed from my face.

"Who is it?" I heard Merri say behind me.

Turning around to look at him, I couldn't speak. Merri's naked body was too hot.

"It's Arny," I eventually told him. "He's saying that I've received two offers with a third from New England pending. One of the offers is for a starting position, and the other is a goddamn lot of money for a backup."

As I told Merri, my phone rang. "Hello?"

"Where'd you go after the showcase? I had a lot of people lined up to meet you," Arny told me, sounding frustrated.

"I had someone I needed to do."

"You mean 'something'?"

"Who wanted to meet me?" I asked, ignoring his correction.

"Everyone. And I need you to get over here."

"Now?" I asked, looking back at Merri.

"Yesterday!"

"I'll be there as soon as I can."

"You better," he said, ending the call.

"He wants me to come by his office."

"Did he say why?"

"No."

"Then you'd better get over there," he said with tired eyes.

Heading back down the hall to the bedroom, I heard, "Should I come with you?"

I turned back to Merri, who seemed to shrink in front of me.

"Of course, you should come with me. Why wouldn't you?" I asked before continuing to the bedroom to get dressed.

Heading to Arny's office, my mind swirled. Was this all happening? It felt surreal. A few months ago, I was sure that I would never play football again. Now, I had offers to play in the NFL. This was amazing!

Parking and hurrying up to the penthouse, I found my agent a little more disheveled than he had been at the Hall of Fame event.

"Have you slept?" I asked him.

"No. And it's because you don't goddamn pick up your phone."

"Sorry about that."

"And where were you yesterday? I can understand taking a break when it was over. But you didn't think to check in with me at all?"

"It won't happen again. Why did you need me here?"

"Because you have to address the media," he said, annoyed.

"What? Why?"

"When a player is a sensation during a showcase and then isn't available for meetings with teams afterward, it creates a bit of a stir. In your case, it's more like a feeding frenzy. You're a fucking hit, Claude. Everyone wants you," Arny insisted.

My heart dropped, stunned. Looking around for Merri's shared excitement, I found him standing meekly in the corner. But I didn't have the bandwidth to figure out what was going on with him. I had a lot to process.

"What do I do?" I asked, turning back to Arny.

"I've arranged for a press conference."

I shook my head in disbelief.

"What am I supposed to say?"

"You know, the usual."

"Which is?"

"I don't know, that you're excited for this opportunity. That you feel you can be a great addition to any team. Talk about how long you've been working for this and make up something about your mother. Anything will do. The press eats up that shit."

Waiting nervously as the reporters gathered, I sat next to Merri. When he didn't say anything, I took his hand for comfort. He was just tired, right? He didn't look like he had slept. Had I hurt him the night before? I hadn't exactly been gentle as I fucked his brains out.

"You okay?" I asked him, squeezing his hand.

"I'm fine," he said, squeezing back. "I'm here for you," he added with a sad smile.

Still not sure what was going on with him, I looked away, trying to gather myself. I had not practiced talking to the press. I didn't know what could happen or what they could ask. This was new territory for me, and I didn't like being unprepared.

"How does it feel to get so much attention?" the first reporter asked me.

"Like you're here for the wrong person," I said, to their laughter.

"We're not," he replied. "I hear you've already received multiple offers."

"I heard that too. Did you hear where they're from?"

"Where are they from?"

"No, I'm asking you. I have no idea," I admitted, to more laughter.

"My sources say Seattle and Portland. That's a long way from Tennessee."

I thought about that.

"That's a long way from a lot of places," I said, looking back at Merri.

As soon as our eyes met, he lowered his gaze. Oh, that's why he was acting weird. Playing for the NFL would mean an end to what we had. A part of me had known that but I had refused to believe it.

"Are you ready for such a big move?"

"No," I said bluntly. "Not at all."

They laughed again.

"I guess you're going to have to be. Play like you did in the showcase, and you'll have a long career out there."

"I guess," I said, sharing Merri's sadness.

With the press conference over, I rejoined Arny in his office.

"Why didn't you tell me which teams had made the offer?"

"I thought you read it in my texts."

"You sent a lot of them."

"That's because I was trying to get a hold of your ass.

"Anyway, where you choose is up to you. I'm just here to get you the offers. New England would be an interesting prospect because of the history of the franchise. But with Seattle, you'll be able to create your own. Besides, small market teams are always willing to fork out more to get talent. They know no one's going there for the weather."

"Seattle's very far away," I told him.

"Didn't you go to school in Oregon?"

I nodded.

"Then you know. There's a lot of good things about being up there. You could have a great life."

When I didn't respond, he continued.

"Look, I know a lot of this is coming at you all at once. Go home. Talk about it with the people you care about," he said, his eyes bouncing over to Merri. "When you've made up your mind, let me know. Preferably, in the next 24 hours."

"24 hours?"

"You're not the only person these teams are making offers to. They're willing to give you a little extra time because they saw how good you are. But wait too long, and you're gonna be the one left without a seat."

"I understand."

"By the way, there's a scout you should thank for this."

I looked up at Arny, confused. "What do you mean?"

"Jason Rodriguez, do you know him?"

"No."

"I do," Merri said suddenly coming alive. "What did he do?"

"He put his reputation on the line to get Claude that Seattle offer. The same for the Portland one. He seemed very motivated to get you there. If you know him, you should thank him. He fought hard for it."

"He fought hard to get Claude as far away from here as possible."

"He fought to make sure Claude landed with a team," Arny said, correcting Merri.

"I'm sure he did," Merri said, telling me that Jason Rodriguez was his ex.

"Well, thank him for me, if you get a chance," I told Arny.

"You bet."

"If there's nothing else, we're gonna go."

"I'll let you know about New England. But I really think you should be thinking about Seattle."

"Got it," I told my agent before heading to our car.

On the drive home, Merri remained silent. He didn't say anything until we re-entered our apartment.

"This place is a mess," he said, looking around.

"It's not neat," I agreed. "So, Merri, what should I do?"

He looked at me as if struggling with the moment.

"You know what you should do. Didn't Arny tell you to think about Seattle?"

"That's what he suggested. But it's my choice," I said, looking for an answer in Merri's eyes.

"I think you should do what's best for you," he said, unable to look at me.

"Is that what you want me to do?"

Merri winced at my words.

"This is what we've been working for, isn't it?" he said, getting angry.

"It is," I admitted.

"Then you should do it. You should go to Seattle," he told me painfully.

"This doesn't mean the end of us, you know," I said gently.

"Of course not. There's no end to us. Didn't we establish that I have issues?"

I smiled. He still didn't look at me.

"I just don't know how it'll be never sleeping again," he said, beginning to cry.

Unable to hold back a second longer, I wrapped myself around him, pulling him to me. He turned and cried in my arms.

"I don't want to leave you," I told him with tears rolling down my cheeks.

"You have to. This is your dream."

"You're my dream," I told him. "You're the man I've dreamed of on cold, lonely nights. You're all I've ever wanted."

Merri directed his tear-filled eyes toward me.

"But, you need to take this. I can't be the one who keeps you from what you were meant to do. You were born to play football. It makes you feel alive. I know it does. You can't pass up this opportunity, especially for me. You need to do this."

Pulling him tight, knowing what I had to do, I took a breath and said, "I'm gonna miss you, Merri. You mean everything to me."

"I love you, Claude. I have from the moment I saw you, and I've never stopped."

"I love you too, Merri. I always will," I told him as my heart broke, knowing he was right.

"I'm accepting Seattle," I told Arny after a day and night of crying with Merri in my arms.

"Excellent choice! I'll get the ball rolling, and you should be ready to fly up to sign the contract in two days."

"Two days? That's too quick."

"They want you for the second half of preseason. That's how the NFL works. Get ready for it," Arny said before ending our call.

"I have two days," I told Merri, fighting back the tears. "I'm gonna have to fly back to Tennessee and pack my stuff. I'm also going to have to explain to Titus that I'm not going to be back until the offseason."

"When do you have to leave Pensacola?" Merri asked vulnerably.

"Tonight," I realized.

Closing his eyes as if refusing to be sad, he opened them, finding his resilience.

"If you have to leave tonight, then I know what we should do today."

"Were you thinking…" I asked with a suggestive smile.

"I wasn't until you said it. And yeah," he said with a mixture of horniness and melancholy. "But I know what we should do before that."

Stepping into Bluegrass Bourbons, Pensacola's top Tennessee-themed bar, I laughed.

"Seriously, who thought building this was a good idea?" I asked, examining the authentic raccoon skin cap that hung between two whiskey barrel-inspired windows.

"I don't know what you're talking about. From where I'm standing, this seems like the perfect place. There should be one in every state. So, what shots should we do? The authentic Tennessee whiskey or the just as authentic Tennessee moonshine?"

"Well, since I'll need my sight to play football, how about the whiskey?"

"And then work our way up to the good stuff. Got it," Merri said, in the mood to make some truly poor decisions.

"What do we toast to?" I asked when I had the whiskey shot in hand.

"To what I said we would on the day I brought you here. To you playing on a fuckin' team in the NFL."

"I'll toast to that," I said joyfully, tossing back the shot, then regretting it immediately. "I'm not gonna be able to fly tonight," I said with my face twisting into a corkscrew.

"That's what pilots are for," he said, placing another shot in front of me.

That first shot led to two, then three, then... um, whatever number came after three. What I'm saying is, despite our worlds crumbling around us, we had a good time. We were just about to ensure that we would regret every second of this by knocking back a shot of moonshine when Merri's phone rang.

"If it's your ex-boyfriend, don't forget to thank him for me," I told Merri sarcastically.

"Fuck Jason," he replied.

Connecting the call, he answered it, "Fuck you, Jason." He paused. With drunken amusement, he said, "I'm celebrating, Papa!" He paused again. "I know. But didn't you hear? Claude will be the starting quarterback in Seattle."

He paused, listening.

"I don't know." Covering the phone, he turned to me. "Did you sign the contract yet?"

"In two days," I said, holding up two fingers I wasn't sure were mine.

"Not yet," Merri said to the phone. "I can ask him," he said before turning to me. "Do you want to meet with the Cougars before you sign your big contract?"

"Hasn't that owner been a complete asshole to you?" I asked, remembering the stories.

"Yes, he has been. But he's my boss," he reminded me.

"Then yes, I would love to meet with the Cougars before I go."

"You're not gonna get me fired, are you? The management sucks and the team sucks, but... What was I saying, again?"

I pointed at the phone he held inches from his mouth.

"Oops!" he said, laughing. Bringing the phone to his mouth, he repeated it. "Oops!"

"Tell them I'll see 'em," I said, struggling to speak.

"He'll see you."

Merri listened for a moment.

"When are you gonna be there?" he asked me.

"I don't know. When are we gonna be there?"

"We'll be there in thirty minutes," Merri declared before ending the call. Staring at me blankly, he said, "You were the designated driver, right?"

Looking down at the definitely more than three shot glasses in front of me, I called an Uber. On the ride to the stadium, I did my best to sober up. But, for some reason, I just got drunker.

Entering the stadium's executive suites, I had to concentrate to keep the floor level. I did, though. So, when Merri and I entered the owner's office with Coach and who I think was the general manager, I was feeling confident.

"Merri, could you?" the owner said, pointing to the door.

Fuck that, Mr. Power move.

"Coach and whoever you are, could you?" I said, mirroring the owner's gesture.

The two men looked at the owner and then left with Merri. When we were alone, I sat in the chair in front of his desk. Falling a lot further than I expected, I realized that I was sitting lower than he was. The chairs weren't even. What a dick!

"I assume you've been celebrating," the old fart said, trying to be judgmental. But, fuck him.

"I got a starting quarterback offer from Seattle. Hey, remember when Merri brought me in to workout for your team and you were a complete asshole to him… and me. Good times, right?"

The old man squirmed.

"Yeah. About that. Things didn't occur as they could have."

"No shit! You made some veiled homophobic slur and dismissed me."

"You have to understand that wasn't about you."

"You think it being about Merri is better?" I asked the idiot.

"I'm not saying that."

"Then what are you saying?"

"I'm saying that the Cougars could really use a player like you. If you joined us, we could guarantee you a starting spot and a three-year contract."

I nodded, considering it.

"That sounds good. But there's a problem."

"What's that? The Seattle contract? You haven't signed it yet, right? Until it's on paper you can back out at any time."

"No, that's not it. The problem is that I am fucking the hell out of Merri. I mean, we are doing it like rabbits. On the counters, on the floor…"

The old guy squirmed and cut me off.

"What's your point?"

"Against the wall. In the shower," I continued, enjoying making him feel uncomfortable.

"I got it! Is there a point to this?"

I stopped and smiled at him.

"Yes. I'm telling you this because Merri is my boyfriend. It took a long time for me to be able to say that. And now that I am, I'm not gonna stop. He is my boyfriend, and I love that man so much. So, if you have a problem with him working here, then you have a problem with me."

His wrinkly lip twitched, staring at me. I could see his gears turning. If I played here and we won, it would be worth millions, if not billions of dollars to him. But to have that, he would have to accept what he didn't want to, the fact that the love between two men was equal to his own.

"I..." he said, abandoning his thought.

"You what?" I asked confidently, leaning forward.

"I... can accept that," he said, to my surprise.

"You'd be okay with Merri and me acting like any other couple when we're here?"

"Like any other couple, you would need to sign papers removing the company from risk if things between you two went badly. But, yes, I could live with that."

Staring at him shocked, I said, "You must really think I'm gonna make you a ton of money."

He looked at me measuredly.

"I think you would be a fine addition to our team."

"I'll take that as a yes. Send the paperwork to my agent. I'll play for the Cougars. But right now, I need to go celebrate with my boyfriend," I told him, getting up and smiling as I left the office victorious.

"What happened?" Merri asked, with his father looking on.

"Coach," I said, offering him my hand. "It'll be a pleasure to play for you again."

He broke into a broad smile while Merri looked at me stunned.

"We're gonna do some great things, the two of us," Coach said, pumping my hand.

"The three of us will do some great things," I said, looking at the love of my life. Brushing Merri's red cheeks with the back of my hand, I stared into his disbelieving eyes.

"We did it, Merri. I love you," I told him, meaning it with all of my heart.

"I love you too, Claude," he said before I leaned down and kissed him.

Epilogue

Claude

Sitting waiting to connect with Titus and Cali over Facetime, I was nervous. With Cali in New York, a lot had happened since the last time the three of us talked. I wasn't sure how either of them would take it.

"Claude!" Titus said, joining the call first. "How's beautiful Pensacola?" He asked cheerfully.

"It's beautiful," I told him with a smile.

He looked at me strangely. "Well, I don't know what that means."

"You don't know what beautiful means?"

"I don't know what that look you're giving me means."

"Hey," Cali said, his mood clearly lower as he joined the call.

"Cali, how's New York?" I asked him.

"I'm at home," he said stone-faced.

"Okay," I replied confused by his expression. "Anyway, I have news to share."

"So do I!" Titus chimed in, his enthusiasm unaltered.

"So do I," Cali said downtrodden.

"That's funny," I told them. "But I'll go first. It looks like I'll be the starting quarterback for the Pensacola Cougars," I said, unable to hide my excitement.

Titus's face lit up.

"I thought that was off the table!"

"The owner saw the showcase and reconsidered. I'm told that he and I met, and things went well."

"Apparently," Titus said excitedly. "Wait, what do you mean that you were told that you met with the owner? Weren't you there?"

"Long story. And I'm still feeling the hangover. But it means I'll be moving here," I told him nervously.

"Oh," Titus said caught off guard. "Permanently."

"I think so. It's a three-year contract, and Merri's here. So…" I shrugged.

"Merri?" Cali interjected. "You mean the Merri I met?"

"Yeah," I said, still smiling.

"Good for you. I liked him," Cali said, his voice warming a bit.

"So did I," Titus added. "Does that mean you're leaving the business?"

"I'll have my off-seasons, but I don't know where Merri will want to spend them. Maybe it will be better to now think of me more as a silent investor."

"Okay," Titus responded, taking it in. "Well, I'm happy for you. That's fantastic news about the contract and Merri."

"Thanks. I guess practice makes perfect. Or at least, practice makes not awful."

Titus chuckled.

"If that was your news, it's my turn. Cage proposed to Quin."

"No way!" Cali said surprised.

"Yep. Quin asked Lou to be his best man and Lou told me. I'm not sure he was supposed to. So keep it under wraps until one of them tells you, okay?"

"You got it," I assured Titus. "Do you know when they're getting married?"

"Not sure. In a few months, I think. It's gonna be big, though. Marcus is catering. I think the whole town will be there."

"That's wonderful! Good for them," I said, genuinely happy. "Cali, what's your news?"

Cali stared at the screen before lowering his head.

"What's wrong?" I asked him.

Straightening up, he steeled himself.

"Remember when Claude's mom gave us the name of our father?"

"Of course," Titus said while a knot formed in my stomach.

"I said I didn't recognize the name, but that was a lie."

"Okay," Titus replied cautiously. "And how do you know the name?"

"From my first trip to New York."

I thought back to what he told us about that trip. His boyfriend Hil had been kidnapped and he had rescued him.

"And how did you come across his name in New York?" I inquired, my nerves on edge.

"I didn't just come across his name. I met him. I met him in person," Cali clarified, his tone grave.

My and Titus's reactions mirrored each other, stunned silence.

"When?" Titus implored.

"When I went to rescue Hil. Armand Clement, our father, was the man who shot me."

Chilling prickles covered my face hearing Cali's words. I couldn't believe it.

"More than that," Cali continued soberly. "Now we need to rescue him."

*****

Sneak Peek:
Enjoy this Sneak Peek of 'Mafia Marriage Trouble':

Mafia Marriage Trouble
(M/M Romance)
By
Alex McAnders

Copyright 2023 McAnders Publishing
All Rights Reserved

Remy Lyon, a billionaire heir to a mafia empire, has always craved his little brother's best friend, Dillon. He saw the beauty in Dillon that Dillon couldn't see in himself, but because of Remy's princeling status, he didn't dare act on it.

At his father's funeral, Remy has one last chance to claim Dillon as his own. His plans are ruined when Armand Clement, the ruthless crime lord who holds his family's life in his hands, breaks their deal.

Remy had agreed to surrender his father's illegal businesses in return for keeping the legal ones and gaining his family's safety and his freedom. But now Armand wants it all, and that includes Remy's hand in marriage to his spoiled daughter.

Desperate to protect his family and stay close to Dillon, Remy hires Dillon to help him navigate the luxurious yet perilous mafia world he inherited. But their attraction soon explodes into a scorching affair that puts them both in danger.

Will Remy give up Dillon, the only guy who can satisfy him, or defy Armand and risk a war that could expose dark family secrets and change their lives forever?

*****

Mafia Marriage Trouble

"Dillon, I've been in love with you for so long. From the moment I met you, I could never get enough. Every time you came by to hang out with Hil, I wondered if you saw me. So, when I had you so close, when I had everything I ever wanted in my arms, I was the happiest I could ever be.

"When you left me, I tried living without you. I knew by doing it I would keep everyone here safe. But the request was too much. I can't stay away from you, Dillon. I need you. I'm here to tell you that if you'll have me, I will never leave you again."

I gathered my emotions, trying to reign in the overwhelming wave threatening to crash.

"Remy," I began softly, "I left you for a reason. You have to be with Eris. Everyone's life depends on it. And even if it didn't, I can't be the other woman… or guy… or whatever. If I could, I'd do it for you. But I can't. I'm sorry!"

"But that's why I'm here," Remy explained. "I know I can't just walk away from Eris. But I also can't live without you," Remy declared baring his heart. "So I'm here to again ask for your help. I don't have all the answers like my father did. And I'm not him, I can't do this alone. I need the help of the people I love. And I love you."
Read more now

Sneak Peek:
Enjoy this Sneak Peek of 'Serious Trouble':

Serious Trouble
(M/M Romance)
By
Alex McAnders

Copyright 2021 McAnders Publishing
All Rights Reserved

'I could feel the heat of him on me. I could barely breathe. Parting my lips as my heart thumped, I needed to be closer.'

Imagine having to sleep inches from your crush but not be able to touch him because he's "straight" and has a girlfriend.

CAGE
With NFL scouts watching my every move, the last thing I should be thinking about is Quinton Toro, my awkwardly sexy, genius tutor who makes me think about breaking my headboard. I might fantasize about everything about him at night, but I've worked too hard for too long to slip up now.

But if it came down to having him or a career in the NFL, which would I choose? The answer should be obvious, right? Then why can't I get the lustful way he looks at me out of my mind?

I might be in trouble.

QUINTON
The problem with falling in love for the first time is that it makes you do crazy things like think you have a shot with the chiseled quarterback with rippling abs, who is not only focused on going pro, but is straight and has a girlfriend.

He is the one who insists we spend time together. That's got to mean he likes me, doesn't it? Why can't I figure this out?

And, how is he going to feel when he learns how much trouble comes with being with me? The only thing I can hope is that we can figure out a way to be together. But could we do it without me getting my heart broken again?

*****

Serious Trouble

I'm falling in love with Quin. I can't deny it. Even as I lie in the morning light not getting nearly enough sleep, all I could think about was how I could touch him like I did last night.

When I heard him place his hand on the bed between us, I sent out my hand in search of his. I didn't know if I should or if he would want me to, but I couldn't stop myself. I need Quin. I ache to be with him. I feel like I would go crazy without him. And to be so close without being able to wrap my arms around him was torture.

I was about to relieve myself of the painful agony when I shifted and something buzzed. When it did, I realized I was still half asleep because it woke me up. I knew the sound. It was my alarm clock. I had forgotten to turn it off.

It was probably more accurate to say that I wasn't foolish enough to turn it off. Ever since I had met Quin, getting eight hours were impossible. Even if I was in bed in time to do it, alone in the darkness was when I thought about him the most. So to have him here now was like a dream come true.

The alarm buzzed again. Oh right, the alarm. I didn't want it to wake up Quin.

Instead of letting it ring like I usually had to, I popped open my eyes and figured out where I was. I was on the right side of the bed. The alarm clock was on the left. I had to reach over Quin to get it.

Not thinking about it, I straddled the guy beneath me and hit the off button on the clock. With it off, I realized where I was. Although our bodies weren't touching, I was hovering above him. I froze and looked down. He was on his back facing up.

My God, did I want to bend down and kiss him. I was right there. He was so close. And then he opened his eyes.

I stared at him, caught. He smiled, or was it a blush?

"Good morning," he said in a raspy morning voice.

Looking at him, I relaxed.

"Morning," I said getting one more good look at him and then rolling back to my side of the bed. "Sorry about that," I told him.

"No, I liked it," he said smiling ear to ear.

"You liked the alarm?"

"Oh, I thought you meant..." He blushed again. "It was fine. Does that mean we have to get up? It's so early."

"I have to get to practice. It's a long drive."

"Okay," he said squirming his body adorably.

Watching him settle, I was about to get up when I noticed something. I had a serious morning wood situation going on. Sure, I was only too happy to show him my hard dick last night. But, I was so turned on by being with him that I had lost all inhibition.

After a night's sleep, as short as it was, I wasn't so bold. Yeah, I was still as turned on as all get out. But, we weren't getting into bed. We were leaving it. That made a difference.

"We could sleep a little while longer, right?" Quin asked facing me, his gorgeous eyes begging for me to hold him.

"You can, but I have to get up. The bowl game's on Saturday. This is our last full practice before it. I can't be late."

"Fine," Quin said disappointed.

Staring into his eyes I tried to think of the next time I could get him back here.

"Do you want to come to the game? Have you ever been?"

"You want me to come to your game?" He asked with a smile.

"Yeah. Why wouldn't I?"

"I don't know. I thought it might be your manly space or something."

"Manly space?"

"You know, a place for your girlfriend and all of your football friends to meet and do football things."

"First of all, the stadium seats 20,000 people. There's room for everyone. Second of all, Tasha hasn't been to one of my games in I don't know how long. You should come. That way you can see what all the fuss is about."

"I can see what all of the fuss is about from here," he said making my heart melt.
Read more now

*****

www.ingramcontent.com/pod-product-compliance
Lightning Source LLC
LaVergne TN
LVHW041753060526
838201LV00046B/988